GW00722408

Echoes

from the

Lost Ones

by
Nicola J. McDonagh

30127080343671

This is a work of fiction. Names, characters, places and events portrayed in this book are either products of the author's imagination or are used fictitiously. Any character resemblance to actual persons, living or dead, is entirely coincidental.

Echoes from the Lost Ones
Book 1 of *The Song of Forgetfulness*

Published by Fable Press
FablePress.com

Copyright © 2013 by Nicola J. McDonagh

All rights reserved. Except for use in any review, the reproduction or utilization of this work, or portions thereof, in any form is forbidden without written permission.

Cover by Rob Allen for n23art

ISBN: 978-1-939897-04-6

First Edition: July 2013

To Martin for his faith in me. To Ian for his encouragement and guidance, and to Sasha and Sarah.

CHAPTER 1
Kyboshed in the Underbrush

Something tiptoed down my back. I clenched my teeth so as not to yell "Yak" and continued to crawl. My hands touched squish and prickle and bugs swarmed around my fingers and neck. I was being chomped by all things natural and I wasn't even a gnat's breath away from the perimeter fence. I knew nowt about the Wilderness, except it was full to brimming with beasties that craved my flesh.

When far enough away so as to be no more than a speck in the distance, I stood and shoulder wriggled until whatever trickled through my flesh hairs fell off. I looked to the sky and with the sun on my right, headed north into the thick herbage; legs heavy from the vegetation that clung to my shins and ankles.

The shrubbery gave way to towering trees crammed so tight that after a few steps I was surrounded by dark. Slim streaks of light slashed through the branches and I was able to see enough so as not to trip over the massive gnarled roots that spread across the ground like giant oldie fingers. I took in a breath of leaf rot and made my way all hush-hush through the forest, ears wide open for sounds of danger.

A snap to my left caused me to stop 'bruptly. I turned my head in the direction of said noise. All quiet. I was skittish to be sure not knowing if wolfie or Agro were on my trail. Another crick-crack, but from the right. I waited for a sec, and then darted into the most densely packed part of the wood. The sound did not follow.

My lower bits began to pulse. Santy Breanna told me once that pain was merely a mind jest and if I forced my will to block it out, then it would cease. So I focused on my purpose; to find my bro-bro, and hoped that she was right.

She was not.

My thoughts turned to the soothers in my backpack and I peered into the gloom in search of somewhere to rest. An unruly hairshambles of a plant high enough for me to squat behind became my hideout whilst I rummaged through my Synthbag and took out a bar of Sterichoc and a killpainpill. Crouched and aching in the prickly vegetation, I swallowed down the tab, scoffed the confec and waited for the goodliness to take effect. I shuffled position and wedged myself deeper into the fronds. It was a robust shrub and I quite believed that I was safe, until the ground began to tremble. I looked through the leaves and saw a whole flock of legs of the male kind coming my way.

I felt a calloused hand grab onto my wrist and haul me into the relative light. His grip was strong but not as much as the pong that drifted from the cluster of raggedy youths that I was surrounded by. I turned my head upwind and pulled myself free of the dirt-faced juve. He jumped in front of me, eyeballed my choc and tried to snatch it from my hand.

I punched him in the face and he staggered back.

No one takes my sweetie things, no one. Especially when I'm going through the redness. I figured that was what attracted them to me. Santy said that they sniff us out like wolfies. Can't but help themselves, living apart from women-folk the way they do.

The teen bared his teeth, made a back-throat snarl and lunged. I sidestepped and he stumbled into the trunk of a tree. Whilst he was occupied with rubbing his injured snout, I sidled away ready to run. But hands unknown grabbed my hair and pulled. I reached behind and dug my fingernails into skin. They yelped and let go. I fell to my knees and scrabbled back to the bush to retrieve my Synthbag. I thrust my fingers into the shrub and felt around until I touched something non-organic. I slipped my hand into the strap and dragged it out. But before I could put it back on, the slit-eyed, teeth-bearing teenmales encircled me.

Some hiss-whistled through half opened mouths. Some cracked their knuckles. Some licked their wet lips and all gave off a sickly urge-filled stink. I turned and turned, looking for a gap in the wall of teen, but they packed tighter together. I noticed them give each other a sly droop-eyed look, nod their heads, then slow step towards me. I thought my chest would explode so fast and hard did my heart thud against my ribcage. The juves crept closer. With nowhere to run, I raised my fists ready to slug it out.

A loud whistle sound stopped their advancement. I heard the thump, thump of feet on dry leaves and the not-yet 'dults stiffened. Two mud-caked hands pushed through the barricade and a thick-waisted male stepped forward. He released a loud, wet snort, and they backed off, breaking the circle. It was a good job the 'dult turned up when he did or I'd be but floor pelt for sure. Those teens looked pretty fierce all right, with soil splattered on their cheeks, necks and foreheads; their eyes staring wild and full of threat. Bits of greenery and twigs stuck out from their matted hair and if I didn't know better, I would think them part tree so much of the forest clung to their bods. Even me, the Roughhouse Champ, would be no match against all of them.

I'm tough but not stupid.

I recognised the one who tried to pinch my choc. He stood opposite me clenching and unclenching his fists. I saw his knuckles turn white each time his fingers bent, and when I caught his eye, he glared back. The others thrust their shoulders forward ready to pounce. I squatted all quick, arms around my head to shield me from a full on attack.

"Pull back ye bulls. Abide by the guidelines," the 'dult said and fanned them away with an air swipe. He turned and gestured for me to stand. I did. He walked over, folded his arms and moved his gaze up and down my bod. "Ye, ye are not one of us."

I slowed my breath so as to appear all-calm like, and answered in a voice without quiver. "Well, nah. Visibly so," I said, and then brushed some dirt from my pantaloons.

"From Cityplace?"

"Goodly guess."

"No guess. Ye attire is crafted machine wise?"

"Surely so."

"Not suited for this rugged terrain."

"That I am discovering with every shoe weary step."

"And yer eyes are of that peculiar blue that only the softies have."

"I am no softie."

"Perhaps not, but ye resemble them in pale of skin and light of hair."

The not-so-big 'dult, for he was no more than a finger joint taller than myself, scratched underneath the filthy pouch that hung around his pleated skirt and said, "Name, girlie."

I had hoped to end this chittle-chat without resort to mention of my moniker.

"Relinquish yer name or I will let the Nearlys have their frolic."

"Let them try," I said and put up my fists again.

"Wirt, what is she called?"

A flimsy looking youth with long straggly brown hair approached and looked between him and me. Then he stared into my eyes, blinked twice and backed away.

"Wirt! Name!"

"Adara," he said, and hung his head as if in shame.

"So that's who yer are girlie?"

"Yes, but I'm no girlie."

"That I can see," he said and stared straight at my bosoomies. "A mistake I'll not make twice."

"May I know your tag?"

"Aiken, and do not forget it."

"Not likely just yet, since we are surrounded by your namesake," I said and pointed at the huge oak trees that loomed above our heads.

The grubby teens grinned and the 'dult male rubbed his food encrusted grey beard. "Adara. That means catcher of birds. Ye will be of use. Ye will enter our domain and deliver yer potential."

That's why I hate saying my name. Every huffin' time they come out with the same thing, like I'm this mythical girlygig who goes around grabbing birds out of the sky so they can eat meat. I AM NOT! It's just a name. A name that well suits me I grant you. Nonetheless, I avoid the broadcasting of it to one and all, save this kind of thing occurs. Tried to give a false one to the Flashlighters once, but they had a Namer there like this Wirt and I had to run quick-quick to avoid being nabbed.

"It's been more than a while since any of us tasted of the beastie. These teens never, not in all their short lives. Ay, ye will be welcome, most rightly. Adara, Auger. Adara, Bringer. Adara, catcher of-"

"Birds, yes I know and I'd be thankful if you could refrain from repeating both my name and its meaning."

"Ye should be proud. Ye have a gift."

"And a curse. Everyone who finds out wants a piece of me."

"Fret not. We only want yer voice, lassie. Give that to us without fuss and ye will keep the rest intact. So, now ye will come with us and do our bidding."

I did not respond. Best not to. Best to let them presume I will abide by their request with my silence. Although an interruption such as this could scupper my mission, there was a chance that the Agro or whatever it was that pursued me would lose the scent.

"Show the Bringer to our home, laddies. And do not peek at her best bits or ye'll be munching on moss for a month."

I pulled my arm away from a particularly low-browed bull, bent down and hitched my Synthbag up over my shoulder before it was noticed. Once in its proper place and invisible again, it discreetly melded into my back leaving my hands free, in case I needed to use them. Santy Breanna was not eager for me to travel on my lonesome, but to whom could I turn? She was broken-boned from the latest skirmish with the Agros when they came to free the Praisebee's and snatch my bro. Plus, there are no shifty pathfinders in Cityplace. Nah, I am best alone. I creep and peep more wisely without the hindrance of a low-grade scout, despite this wooded area being an alien topography. Oh I stared at the downloadliness of the place on Deogol's comp, but that was all 2-D's. This, this was most severely 3-DD!

I walked with the males, who behind Aiken's back took it upon themselves to poke and prod me as they tramped past. I flicked their probing paws away and they took to assuming a most leering look. Some pursed their lips and made a smoochy noise, whilst others let their tongues roll around their mouths. I quickened my pace so as to be nearer to Aiken, my only defender against these lovelorn pubescents.

The thickness of the forest waned a bit and I was able to discern some high up blue. Although dread-filled in the extreme, I found it a comfort when I raised my eyes to discover that the sun was still on my right. It soothed me to think that I was on the correct path despite being hemmed in by panting males. Things buzzed around my face and big-eyed whirling, flappy creatures skidded across my head and arms. I swatted them away and shuddered.

"Babbie, to be feared of the creepy crawlies," a sneer-teen said. The others guffawed loudly and brushed past me as though I were nowt but a swaying twig. I sniffed, squared my shoulders and walked on.

A sound I had not heard since my first try at birdycalling halted the march. I cocked my ear upwards and heard Raptors screech screeching above our heads. I snickered at the so-called 'Nearlymen' when they ducked down and covered their heads with their hands until the circling birds of prey flew off. I stood straight and unflinching, showing them my fearlessness. Never hurts to have the upper udder, as they say.

Especially when there are twice as many of them than you and especially when you're as scared as a birdybird landing on the ground.

Aiken was the first to stand, followed by the rest, who coughed and slapped their thighs to indicate they lacked sissyness. The 'dult pointed his stubby finger at a tall, slim juve, who gulped and looked over his shoulder.

"Gifre, yes ye laddie, run on ahead and let Brennus know what's what."

"Aye Aiken, I'll travel swift," the teenbull said and ran away from us.

"See that ye do. A catch like this is proper welcome. Particularly in these hungry times."

His words caused me to take a long look at the scrawny males around me. The bulkiness of their clothes made them look all-broad and muscle bound. But I caught the sight of collarbones protruding from their shirts. I put my hand on the pulled-tight belt around my trousers, stared more deeply at my unwelcome companions and recognised the look of want in all their sallow faces. No wonder my presence was well sought after.

"We walk silent so as not to entice the wolfies. Wirt, keep the rear," Aiken said. I followed behind the slow moving machos afraid of both hound and Agro alike.

"Sorry."

"What?" I said and turned my head. The Nearly called Wirt galumphed his way towards me. The long sleeves of his too-big green tunic flapped around his arms and I saw how thin his wrists were. He gave me a sadly grin and I could not help but offer back a look of forgiveness so earnest was the face he presented. He came up alongside me and took several sneaky peeks, before I stopped ready to swipe.

"Apologies. I did not mean to peer so. It's just that I have never seen a Bringer before, or been so close to one with such power."

I lowered my fists and patted Wirt on the shoulder. A cloud of dirt puffed into the air and I caught a whiff of something not quite fresh. They have a smell these teens. It's not a nice pong, not nice at all.

"Ye wrinkle yer nose at my unwashedness."

"No, yes, sorry. It's just that where I come from such musky a scent does not filter though to trouble our senses much."

Wirt sniffed his own armpits and frowned. "Ye have never seen dirt before?"

"Of course. Just not at home. My ma and pa were always clean. So scrubbed spotless that no damn virus could touch them. Or so they thought. Too squeaky for their own good, that's what Santy Breanna said. Suppose she was right. First trip to the edge of the Beyondness, they catch a cold. My guess is you and yours fight infection with a layer of grime."

"Rightly so. It has been our way ever since the Lastgreatplague. Nay, look, we have lagged behind. Will ye follow on fast?" I nodded and we hurried after the rest.

The trees became dense, so much so that I could not distinguish between trunk and twisted vine. The Bulls fairly sped on ahead. Running over the muddy, thorn-ridden ground, as though it were strewn in fine hand-woven mats. I stepped more heedfully, ducking from low branches that swiped at my face when a Nearly pushed his way through.

"What brings ye into our territory?" Wirt said low into my ear.

I do not know why, but I felt that he was a trustworthy sort, and I blabbed in full my one and only purpose.

"I come in search of my bro-bro and the Agro who stole him; and mark my words, those who think me weak and feeblewomb, I will find and kill the crotchless clod. See if I don't."

"A worthy mission, but I am surprised ye mam and da let ye travel alone."

"I was a tot when they died, and my bro-bro still sucking."

"I am sorry for ye loss. Ye must miss them greatly."

"Not so much. The only thing I remember about them was that they always smelled freshly washed."

"When one so close to us no longer roams, the tribe decides where their nearest and dearest shall next abide. Did the Cityfolk do same for ye and yers?"

"Cityfolk do not care about anyone but themselves. Too caught up in their own sterile world, too afraid they might catch something off someone else to stress themselves about the fate of two young 'uns orphaned."

A crick-crack noise to my left caused me to stop. I swivelled round expecting to see a movement in the undergrowth, but all I saw was a teenbull hitching his skirt up so that he could piss against a tree. I shuddered at the thought that there was nowhere for him to wash his hands, then shuddered again when I saw him wipe said dirty mitt across the front of his chest. Wirt shrugged his shoulders and rolled his eyes, then came up close.

"What became of ye after yer parents died?"

"Santy Breanna took us in and introduced me to all kinds of buggalugs. Not in the place we lived of course."

"What? Ye were raised by one of 'The Special Army of the Neworld Territories?'"

"No, I wish. Santy Breanna was destined now to live with us in our Cityhome"

"She must have missed the nomadic life some?"

"Rightly so I guess, but she did take us on camping trips into the one-and-only park. The times spent amongst the greenly stuff was apt. Made me strong, made me almost as brave as she. Her name suits. For she is the bravest female I have ever known, but then she used to be Backpacker in the Beyondness."

"I have heard of these Backpackers. Aiken said that they do not fear the Agros."

"'Bout only folk that don't. When I am of age I too wish to be a Backpacker and give the Agros a taste of my fists."

I felt a sharp thud in the middle of my back and turned to see Aiken all narrow-eyed. He put a finger to his lips. "Sshh. Do not make so much noise. Wolfies abound hereabouts. Move without chitter-chatter."

"My fault, wiser man. I engaged the auger in-"

"That I do not doubt. Ye have a sissified way with ye to be sure. Now tramp silent or ye will be punished."

I saw Wirt wince at Aiken's words and found myself warming to this friendlier than the rest juve. A rush of derisive chuckles rippled through the other bulls and Wirt's face became as bright as the rising sun. For one of not too dissimilar an age as myself, I regarded his embarrassment as my own and made an effort to keep him close. He had a way of moving that was unlike the others, a less bulky waddle that made him look as graceful as a leaf swaying in the wind. I snickered at my own poetic turn of phrase. Wirt turned his head, glanced at my cheesy grin and showed me his discoloured teeth. At least I'd found one Nearly who wished nowt from me but chat.

CHAPTER 2
Rough Night Amongst the Nearlymen

All the while we trudged I listened for sounds of Agro. On my own not so hard, but with all these teens plid-plodding heavily, I found it impossible. Plus, sort of hard to concentrate on said task whilst constantly smacking their probing paws off my behind. I walked closer to Wirt and the Nearlys kept their distance. The trees began to thin a bit and I was able to get a better look at my surroundings that were so different from Cityplace. Everything there was made from metal and concrete, all so geometrically perfect, and all so bland and cold. Here there was variation on a goodly scale.

I began to take an interest in the place they were taking me to, and whispered into Wirt's ear, "Is it true that you live inside charred trees?" He nodded and I continued, "I saw one in a photomag. Wow and then some. It was decorated with feathers and greenly stuff and looked like a present waiting to be unwrapped." He smiled and I looked around to see if I could detect one of these organic abodes.

Nope, nadder. I didn't see any such places in this forest. Only thing I saw was giant curly leaf things and spiky ground twigs that caught my ankles and made them bleed. The nick to my shins hurt, but not so much as the ache in my innards that came not from the monthlies but from the loss of Deogol. All I wanted to do was to get back on track and find my bro. This abduction by the Woodsfolk males was not part of my hastily put together plan. I peered from side to side in an attempt to determine if there was a way to rid myself of them and thought I saw a means to do so, in the shape of these bulls losing concentration and marching ahead all in one glob, almost as if my presence had been forgot.

Just when I was about to create a diversion and somehow make good my escape, we came upon a clearing. Light shone down and I was able to get a proper look at this new landscape. I'd never seen so many different sorts of trees, and they were alive. The ones in Cityplace were near dead or as good as. Their magnificence blew away all thoughts of previous escape and I turned and turned looking up into their dark canopies. I couldn't help myself; I had to touch one. I swear when I did I felt its heart beat. I wanted to snuggle under it, to dig amongst the dry brown leaves, to delve into the soil and touch its finger roots with my own - but Aiken swatted my hand away and pushed me forward.

I fell down, but quickly recovered and sat back on my heels. I looked up and saw a real big Manlyman standing over me. He wore a faded red tunic and black plaid wrap skirt that came to his knees, which were as big as a moocows. I guessed he was in charge 'cause all the other males bowed their heads, crossed their chests with their arms and chanted, "Brennus! Brennus! Brennus!" I rose and stood before him, chin out, hands on hips, careful to hide my extra fingers by keeping them behind my back; and in said pose showed him I wasn't afraid. Inside I quivered like a dewdrop on a web and felt stinky sweat trickle down my back.

"Catcher of Birds, it is an honour to have ye close to our Nearlymen and Manlymen. Tonight ye guest with us as one of our own. Next day ye bring meat to our sitting downs."

I puffed out my chest in defiance, and caught sight of Wirt from the corner of my eye. He stood further back from the rest and when I turned towards him, he shook his head and frowned. I gleaned more information about the state of things from his sad expression than if I had shouted at him to tell me all about this burly male. Clearly there was no point in arguing with this Manbull. So I folded my arms and nodded, to indicate that I would carry out his wishes, knowing full well that I would do nothing of the sort. Brennus raised his arms and head and let loose a shriek of high proportion. I felt myself being picked up and thrown over the shoulder of a Nearly. He carried me all-a-bobbing out of the clearing and into the biggest Homeoak I'd ever seen.

He stopped at the entrance, which was nowt but a large hole with a heavy, brown coarse cloth hanging over it. I squiggled myself free of the unwashed Nearlyman and smoothed down my tunic. It had ridden up higher than I would have liked during my ungainly transportation. He huffed and puffed and murmured in my general direction.

"Ye are heavier than ye look."

"And you are weaker than you should be," I said and turned my back on the rudeness of the teen. Not his fault though. He was right, I was heavier than I seemed due to my invisible Synthbag, which was crammed full of necessities and stuff to help me on my travels. I would not dare reveal that I owned such a precious and valuable thing to these oafs.

When I had recovered from my insult I pulled the makeshift door to one side and stepped in. I hadn't expected such a dull exterior to have such a cheerful and bright interior. It was one big round room lit by fizzing tar sticks stuck in the floor. Their light made crazy shadows that danced and twitched like ghosties on All Hallows Eve. The dandiest woven grass mats in all kinds of colours lay here and there on the ground. There were shelves jutting out from the walls of the tree trunk, with stiff hammock-like beds nailed onto them and in the centre was a great fire with black smoke rising up and billowing out from a hole at the top. I counted twenty-six Nearlymen and five Manlymen gathered around the fire. All were sitting on thick rugs, supping something hot from clay bowls. A cauldron swung above the flames attached to a tripod made from what looked like old bits of rusted metal bars. The smell that oozed from it was goodly and my stomach gave out an impetuous growl.

"Come Bringer, sit and share our grub," Brennus said.

I cast my eye about in search of Wirt as I had lost track of him when I was lugged into the place. I spied him standing beside one of the light sticks near the entrance, all alone without any food, his head bowed and his feet tracing circles in the dust. A low chuckle filled with lech escaped from the dribble mouth of a Nearly sat opposite to where I stood. The rest of the teenbulls had a look of yearn and I swear I could hear their nads contract when I moved towards the sitting 'dults. I pulled my Synthowool cape tighter across my chest and sat amongst the Manlymen. They stared at my face and down belows, and I quickly crossed my legs. If I believed in the Greenman I would have prayed for his protection. But I don't, so I just sat and ate the stew they gave me, hoping I would be safe.

The fire spit spat and sent flecks of gold embers spurting around the room. When I was just a tot and on my first camp with Santy, she made a fire and I thrilled to the sputtering of logs and the flashes of cinders as the wood cracked and faded. I thought they were the eyes of the dead keeping watch on those that still prevailed. Santy Breanna just smiled when I said this to her, but you know what? She didn't say it wasn't so.

I continued to nosh and peruse the place, wondering how they kept dry if it were to rain. I looked up and noticed that the hole at the top had a canopy pulled half way across it with two ropes descending to a massive hook stuck near the bottom of the wall. No doubt the thing could be pulled over in case of a downpour. I glanced back to where Wirt stood, head bent as if he were not allowed to lift it up. I wondered why he did not join the rest, and then saw Aiken approach him, scuttling like an earwig in the shadows. He peeked around the room and I lowered my gaze, but not enough so that I could not see what he was doing. He whispered words into Wirt's ear that made the youth close his eyes and grimace and me to further question the actions of these males. Wirt shook his head and Aiken gave him a mighty cuff around the ears, which made him totter forward. Then the 'dult walked slinkily back and set his backside down next to Brennus.

"The hour is overdue and I would see ye lay down. A bunk up high should keep ye right till morning. Don't frown. The fire crackles endlessly. No wolfies dare come near," Brennus said with a look of softness I had not believed possible on a face so marred with struggle and lack of soap. I did not have the heart to say it wasn't the wolfies that made me fret, but the Nearlymen and their burning eyes.

"Do you think I could have some water to abloosh myself with before I take to bed?" A hush fell upon the place, and all cast down their eyes as though I had said "Schmallenberg infection."

"Such luxuries are forbidden. We roll in dust and wipe our lower bits with moss. Ye are welcome to do the same."

"Oh, ta," I said and felt a gush of heat swarm over me. I noticed that the Nearlys all had a leering look upon their gobs. Some, I swear, had their hands below their skirts. The heat fastly turned to an icy shiver and I feared for my safety. Brennus frowned at the foolish grins and low guttural barks that emitted from the gathered males, and clicked his tongue between his yellow teeth.

"Desist from conducting yerselves like lovesick Monks and think of higher things. Preferably above the waist," he said and clapped his massive hands.

Wirt appeared and I felt a burst of relief sweep over me. I took a closer look as he approached. In the gloom of outside, I had not been able to eye him clearly. I hadn't realised just how odd he was from the rest. His face was cleaner than the others and his fingernails were smooth, as though a girlygig had given him a handcare.

"This teenbull will take ye to the place of wash and help ye to yer resting." Brennus leant close and spoke in lowness so only I could hear. "This male is too fine for what he must become. Ye womb is safe, be soothed by this."

I picked up some meaning from his remark, his Highland accent as thick as all the others meant I had some difficulty in comprehending all that he said in one go. It was the word "safe" that finally caused my muscles to slacken. I showed respect and bowed, then turned toward the not-right teen. He gave me a tiny smile, and for reasons I know not, I took his hand and said, "Show me where you splosh." His face went redder than a bub about to plop and everyone, including me, let out a merry guffaw. I hadn't meant to use such a nursery word, but when I looked at his soft brown eyes and slender arms I went all mumsly. Not like me at all. I began to wonder if the 'dults had palmed a soother into my stew.

"Wirt, take our guest and look to keep yer gaze upwind and hands inside yer pouch."

"I shall be as bro and see no harm come, as is the duty of the colony and Woodsfolk alike," Wirt said and strode dainty-like to the threshold. I followed keenly, glad to be away from the smell of teenbull urge. I took a swift look back and saw three grisly looking Nearlys stare keenly at Wirt. They dug each other in the ribs and nodded their heads. Aiken walked up beside them and whispered who knows what into their ears. I shivered not knowing why and hurried outside to join my escort.

It was dark. Not so strange for nighttimes I know, but in Cityplace the sky is always lit with the glare from road lamps and info boards. I lifted my head to the heavens and saw something wondrous.

Stars.

Millions of them winked and blinked, making shapes that looked like old, old cartooneys that Santy Breanna showed me once. Although I had witnessed these bright objects before when scouting with her, it had been a great lapse of time since I had perused them in all their might. I lost myself in their luminance until Wirt coughed.

"'Scuse yer musings, but it's cold and I forgot to heave on my thigh socks. The place for relieving is quick."

"Right, sorry. Lead me on."

He walked ahead and I could not help but notice how lightly he treaded each step. Although a hand taller than myself and thinner around the middle, he was as graceful as a kittle chasing a nanomouse in a slab-tech game. I kept close and listened for wolfie growls, or Agro steppings. He must have heard my fear and turned.

"No wolfie tonight, too clear and bright. Our Lady Moon protects with her generous gleam."

I had forgotten that the Woodsfolk believe so well in all things Nature, and confess to say, on witnessing the glowy stars, I understand why they just might.

Wirt stopped by an interwoven willow screen and waved his hand to indicate I should go behind. Placing my feet carefully to avoid mushy lumps, whose origin I could only guess at, I slinked behind the concealment and let out a sigh. My bladder bulged beyond its capacity and I badly needed to change my reddie sponge. So I called out to Wirt.

"Is there a special section for bodily fluids to escape?"

"We mainly dig a hole and piss in there."

"Oh, right. I'll just do that then," I said and gouged the ground with the heel of my walkerboots. I loosened my trousers, dropped them, pulled down my Stayclean pants, and filled the hole and then some. Taking Brennus's advice, I snatched some moss from the side of the screen and dried my parts. Then attended to my blood sponge. I did not however, roll around in the dirt, but used a Moister from my Comfort bag to wash away the grime and mud from face, armpits and hands. Feeling as clean as could be expected, I returned to Wirt.

"Better for the relieving?"

"To be sure."

"Then let us to bed. Tomorrow ye must use yer powers and provide us all with…"

He stopped quite sudden and put his hand over his mouth. I froze and heard the puff-puffing of a beast nearby. "Wolfie?" I asked preparing myself for flight.

"No. Keep walking."

I did, but found it hard to keep up with Wirt, who paced speedily without the need to run. The animal noise grew louder, as did the sound of other foots. I was relieved at the thought that more teens or 'dults were with us and slowed to catch my breath.

"Stay with me, do not slack."

There was an urgent tone to his words, which left me quite confused. Until I felt a hand grab my arm and yank me to the ground. I didn't stay there long.

Years of training with Santy Breanna had made me well prepared for scrap. Agro was my first thought, but on rising I noticed the familiar Woodsfolk patterned skirt, worn by the Nearlys and 'dults alike. I became at once feared and disgruntled at their boldness. No male would be taking my most prized, not without my utmost authorisation.

Of that you can be sure.

"Keep to the soil girlie. Our intent lies with him," a larger than the rest male said. I could not help but think that I had heard his voice before. He wound his fingers around Wirt's wrist. "If ye do not comply, yer time will come. Bringer or not."

I stood and saw what passed for three Nearlymen and a Manlyman. Their faces covered with a thin red gauze. To disguise their real and mean intent, no doubt. I was about to rage and take one down when Wirt spoke, "Rest behind the tree and listen to yer digits. I will come for ye when all is done."

"Erh? Wirt, what's up?"

"Do this I say and they'll not partake of yer things. If I return with ye all wronged, then I will be taught a lesson I'll not forget in a hurry."

"Wirt, pull away."

"Please, yer safety is in peril."

"As is yours. I sense it from their hunger."

"Which is of full ripeness. Go, now."

The look of anguish he threw at me, made me back away and do his request. I sneaked behind a great big tree, squatted on the ground and put my fingers in my ears.

CHAPTER 3
Tough Love

I could tell from the leftover wet on his cheek that Wirt was in pain. Inside, and out. There was a small bruise on the side of his full pink mouth and a deep graze on the side of his neck. His red wrap skirt was the wrong way round and the scratch marks on his calve and knees did not come from the greenery with spikes where I'd found him on his hands and knees. On seeing me, Wirt stood.

"We must to camp or the elders will become wary of our absence."

"You shake with hurt. Let me ease the signs of struggle before we leave," I said and set my Synthbag on a moss-covered rock. Wirt let his head hang down and I was overcome with mumsly concern. "Come, sit and I'll swipe a Mediswab across the wounds. The healing is quicker than the ravaging. It is a pity that I only have treatment for the surface aches."

"Not so," he said, sat down next to me and took my hand. His grip was soft and warm and as gentle as a bubs kiss. I squeezed lighter than I'm used to and carefully placed the Mediswabs across the red marks on his legs.

"What they did…"

"Let us not speak of it."

"So many kinds of wrong has happened here Wirt."

"I must not think of it. I must not."

I watched him squeeze his eyes tight shut and breathe in hard. He did a better than good job at preventing the shakes to overthrow his body and despite his delicate ways, I thought him the bravest and strongest male I had ever known.

"You should maybe let Brennus in on what those Thugbulls did."

"The first time, I did so."

"The first? How many more since?"

"Eight, no, nine."

"He would not have this stop?"

"He would not have this voiced."

"Coward."

"No, careful."

"They will not reach manliness this way."

"They already have."

I stood and turned from him, not wanting him to see the anger in my face. I wiped away a tear and breathed in a deep lungful of cold air. "Tomorrow I shall bring meat and more."

"Ye are deep with feeling."

"I am deep with rage."

"Empty it. I have, long ago. Ye see," Wirt said and held up his graceful hands. "They gave me perk. To keep my silence. I am the only Nearly let to puff-puff upon the baccy that blanks things out. Plus, the Ladies when they come to rub the tired and sore limbs of the Manlymen and tell their make believe tales, they make pet of me."

"Clean nails and befuddlement cannot make up for their digression."

"In one year I will be a Manlyman and then I'll leave."

In one year, I thought, this makeshift male will be as nothing. I had a scheme brewing in my nonce. "Are you fit to travel?"

"With yer care I am."

I offered Wirt my arm and he pulled himself upright. I made a smile and swished his skirt to face the right way and to my discomfort and joy, Wirt wrapped his arm around my middle and huggled me close. Now, if any other uninvited teen had done this to me, I would have ripped his nads from their resting place and flung them to the raptors. Instead I did the same to him, and cozied thus, we walked back.

Just before the entrance, Wirt and I dropped arms. He strode in first then I slightly behind. The Nearlymen were all-abed and only Brennus and the greybeard Aiken were still awake, sitting and supping something hot. Wirt approached them and they sent their focus to the floor.

Cowards. Cowards all.

"Safely returned as was bid," Wirt said.

"Job done well. Retire. Go quick," Brennus said without lifting his gaze. Wirt bowed and left. "Catcher of birds, sit one sec more. Will ye try some grog?"

"I do not partake." A lie. I have and dare say will again, but my mistrust for these males ran deeper than the lake at Ness.

"Then sit. I will have words or two."

"Speak. I have no relish of squatting in your midst."

"Understood." He raised his giant head and stared full into my eyes. I gazed back not intending for one jiffy to allow him a win. "Ye were found a distance from yer land. Aiken here, so taken with yer status, omitted to discover yer purpose."

"I quest for my bro-bro, taken by the Agros."

"So, they have reached as far as that? We have heard rumours that Cityplace is under siege from the Agros. Is this true?"

"It is."

"What drove them to set upon ye in such a manner?"

"To free the Praisebee rebels that were incarcerated. And, as it turned out, to filch my bro. Santy Breanna and other Specials took a stance against them and they sent forth troops to put us in our place. The whole city was in lockdown when I left."

"Then how did ye escape?"

"Diversion set up by a S.A.N.T. and an oldie. I shot past the pre-occupied mugs and set fourth directly to the perimeter guards. One gave me a tip off and I headed into the forest before I was missed."

"Why here?

"Not sure. I gleaned not much info from the guard. He just sent me deep into your province as quick as that. I dare say he wished to have me gone before the Agros observed my lack of presence."

Brennus rose to his feet and loomed over me as if to strike. I held my position, ready to kick at his delicate area.

"Sent here? For what purpose?"

"That he did not declare."

"What did he say?"

"That answers would be forthcoming."

"Nay more?"

"Nope."

"Ye are yet of youth. To be travelling alone is not without question."

"I have years enough to clear me for solo duties. And I am well trained from my Santy Breanna."

"A S.A.N.T. gave ye school?"

"For many a moon and sun. Twelve to be exact."

"And how old when ye started?"

"Four and three quarters."

Aiken wolfed down his grog and stifled a mild "Ha, ha, ha." Brennus changed his look of threat to one of kindred and slapped me on the shoulder. Sending my camouflaged Synthbag to the floor. I quickly scooped it up before they got a glimpse. Everyone, despite their choice of dwelling, knows about the goodies contained within and I did not want to be severed from their comfort.

"Very well, little warrior, very well. To bed and rest for tomorrow ye will be sorely set to test. We will feast upon the meat ye provide for many a long day."

I did not like the last part of his speech. It indicated my stay would not be brief. "I cannot give vent that much. I am bound to limit the numbers lest there be no more to dine upon." Brennus did not respond. "If I were to annihilate too many birdybirds that would mean extinction, and extinction means…no more meat. Ever."

"We shall see. There are more than enough to go round in these parts. Our kin have not had taste of flesh since before my coming out. The Agros have slimmed our rations too. Nae so long past, a gaggle of Agro brutes swarmed into the women-folk's camp and set about smacking and slapping. My own comfort mate was gashed about the head and legs. When word reached our ears we fled quick as quick to find all manner of tears and sighs, our homes all broken and soiled. Kiddles and old 'uns shivering in fear as they washed away the blood from their wounds. The women fought back as best they could, but they have no proper weapons and young 'uns were took."

"Yep, sounds about right. Agros only attack those least able to defend themselves. The cutting back of foodstuffs is a coward's way to weaken those they wish to overcome. Provisions have dwindled in Cityplace too, and when I left all means of power had been severed."

"I cannot say how ye and yers will manage, but if me and mine are to survive their nefarious scheming, we have to live by our wits and yer talent. I think ye will be staying long. Ye will bring a swarm of relief to our plagued peoples."

Not on your turgid waste, I wanted to shout for all to hear, but all I did was grunt in way of acquiescence. But then an image of Deogol flashed into my noggin and I blurted out, "And yet, I must retrieve my stolen bro."

"There will be time for that and more. Do not fret for yer lost one. There is feeling in the wind that those that have been took are not damaged."

"This is something feasible?"

"Word from those who know would say it is."

"Then I must take your side of things as truth."

"Good. All is set. The cot up high where the ladder rests is to be yer space whilst ye are here. Sleep without thoughts," he said and bowed.

I gave a curt nod and headed towards the ladder. I do not like the highness of things especially when I can see no enclosure to stop a drop. I scanned the sleeping teens all wrapped up like babybubs and climbed the long, long ladder. The highest place I'd ever been was the middle of an info board in the main plaza, and then I'd taken an antivertigo pill. This ascent was more than ten times that height and my legs wobbled all the while. The platform reached, I wiped my brow and tried to not look down. The bed to my relief was secured with massive clamps. I gave it a goodly shake to make sure it was safe, then climbed between the Flexisheets and relaxed a little as they moulded into shape around my body. I breathed in deeply, closed my eyes and opened them again. Thoughts of sleep in this shifty place sent a wave of hot and cold up and down my spine.

I moved my head to the side and looked down the rungs of the ladder for signs of teen. All was clear. I did not doubt that Brennus meant me no harm, but I feared that once he was dream-filled, my safety would be in jeopardy. I vowed to stay awake lest a creepy Nearly ascended and fiddled with my bits whilst I slept. I stared at the hole in the roof, at the swirling smoke and embers that drifted through and felt my lids grow heavy. I lifted them half way but gravity had other ideas. They fluttered briefly, then fell.

CHAPTER 4
The Day of Getting Even

I thought my head was somewhere else when I awoke. It swam and tumbled as though I were hanging upside down. I squeezed my eyelids together, and the up and downess faded. Altitude sickness. I fumbled amongst the tight sheets and came upon my Synthbag caught around my feet, which I unravelled and nimbly opened up. I took out a Soother, placed it on my temple and sighed as it sank into my brain. All better, I rose in near darkness as it was not quite time for the moon to be forgot. In such dimness I gave myself up to curiosity. I wriggled free from the constraining bedclothes, knelt, gripped onto the edge of the platform, and saw row after row of snoozing teenbulls. In the flattering light they looked all innocent and noble.

I came over all-woozy, leant against the wall to compose myself and got a feel of its texture. Several knots dug into my back and I moved myself over their gnarled surface, positively sighing with relief as the knobs scratched itch after itch I didn't even know I had. I let out a sigh, then remembered Wirt's anguished face and the marks of ruffing up upon his soft flesh. Out there all a-cosy and sleeping the sleep of the blameless, were several males as guilty as an Agro filching a bub.

I bit my tongue before a yell of "sissy's all" escaped from my lips, and noticed a grey-bearded figure mosey towards the sleeping Nearlys. My high position made it difficult for me to see exactly where he was headed. I raised myself slowly, so as not to allow the altitude to get the better of me again, and stood. I inhaled the smell of corruption that swirled around the room like smoke from a dreampipe. The 'dult fairly reeked of skank design as he scuttled amongst the resting teens. A red-hot anger began at my toes and crept up and up my limbs until all I could think of was revenge.

Time for me to keep my promise and fetch them all some beastie flesh.

Quiet as a Monk's fart, I slithered down the ladder and tiptoed outside. Gaining in belief of my unseen exit, I hid behind a tree, dug a hole in the dirt and made a much-needed plop. This outdoor toilet doings was not something to be relished, but there being no indoor means of relief; I hardened my finer sensitivities and thought it good experience for when I began training as a Backpacker. I kicked some dead leaves over my droppings, took off my Synthbag, pulled out a Moister and refreshed my sleep-blocked face. Then unplugged myself, noting that my sponge was dry and the reddiness a thing to not think about until next month.

The ground had a light frost upon it and a hazy mist twisted around my legs. I would have to wait until the sun sucked it up before I sang my song. I could not afford said fogginess to stick upon my vocal chords and diminish the intensity of my tune. They named me well although I do deny it. Although, I fight against it. I am "The Catcher of Birds" and as it is my calling, I must do right by it and poor Wirt. They would have their meat and choke upon it.

I headed back to the Oakhome and saw Wirt dart from the entrance. Aiken chased after him, his skirt all hanging loose.

Son-of-a-Peado!

I raced after, taking a vombomb from my trouser pocket. I hurried close enough to see Wirt stagger and fall. Aiken, mitts all ready, kicked him in the ribs and spat upon his face.

"Coward!" I shouted and threw.

The tiny ball landed on his neck and burst. Aiken swatted at the entry point thinking it perhaps a gnat. But I knew better and so did Wirt. When Aiken's mouth dropped open and he squirted up his guts, I ran to Wirt and pulled him up. His nose was all bloodied and there was a gash across his cheek. I turned to Aiken who by now was lying on the ground twitching and clutching at his belly. He groaned and writhed and I spat upon his face.

"What have ye done?"

"Nothing that won't wear off before too long."

"They'll come for me. They'll teach me a lesson. They'll…" Wirt didn't finish his speech. He fell to his knees and blubbed and blubbed. I knelt beside him and took his shaking hands in mine.

"It's nearly time for me to get some meat. When I do, stay close. So close we are as one. You will do this?" By way response, he laid his head upon my shoulder. "Good. Now we must go back."

"But they'll know. Aiken will be missed."

"Not so much. If they ask, I'll say I saw him go for plops."

Wirt raised his head and despite the muck and spittle that ran down his chin, he gave a whisper of a smile to me. I wiped his face with the sleeve of my tunic, rummaged in my Synthbag and handed him some Sterichoc.

"Ye sure ye want to part with such a treasure?"

"Keep shutums about this. It's sterichoc."

"I believed that to be a lie."

"No, all true. Self-replicating choc. Or it would be, if I had the DNA and the 3D imaging device. But I have enough to keep me indulged for a while, I think"

Wirt sniffed the sweetness and gulped it down in one.

"Such meltiness and sweet-sweet flavour. This truly is a wonder of wonders."

"Time for glorifying later. Up we get," I said and we walked back to Oakhome, the groans of Aiken fading in the mist.

We paused outside the entrance. I peered in through a small gap in the cloth hanging and saw the males sitting around the cauldron, eating. I squeezed Wirt's hand for a sec and went inside. The great fire whooshed with warmth when we entered and a pleasing smell of oatly's wafted towards us. Both our guts grumbled with hunger. Wirt took his place next to a hairy-faced teen, grabbed himself a bowl and ladled a great splat of the porridge into it. Brennus lifted his head and gestured for me to sit.

"Welcome Adara. Here, eat our humble chow. Then set to work."

"Don't mind if I do," I said all bold. He handed me a large portion. I took it, sat next to him and scoffed down the proffered goo.

"What tune will ye sing to bring down the birdybirds?"

"The only one I know. Not much to choose from since their voices are not so often heard, what with them being so aloof. They tend not to hover close to where those that would capture and eat them dwell. Santy Breanna told me once, that birdies used to land and folk would put out food for them to feed upon."

Brennus laughed and slapped his thigh. "Today we eat meat! Today we frolic with the knowhow of having ourselves a real life birdy catcher. Others will take note and our tribe will be great and honoured. Ladies will flock to our abode once more!"

A great cheer and clanging of bowls ensued to Brennus's false claims. I caught Wirt's eye and gave a look as if to say "Get ready" and stood. All rose with me and Wirt clip clopped to my side. I waved my hand in the air and hurled my breakfast bowl against the wall. It smashed in two and all gave out an excited whoop and walked towards where I stood. I stayed them with a raised open palm and began to sing.

I warbled loud and clear, a savage sound that came from beneath my bowels. The fire retreated back inside itself, as though scared of what was to come. I backed away towards the opening, felt Wirt's fingers grip tightly at my pants and raised the volume. The males turned white when my singing reached an almost scalding intensity. I stepped outside and felt the cold air bite into my skin

The sun had risen and dried up the ice and haze revealing swirling black dots high above our heads. I softened my trills so as to listen to the song of the gathering birdybirds. I gazed upon their swirling shapes, free and boundless and wished that I could see them all up close and watch them peck and frolic.

My sentimental musings ended when the males appeared armed with clubs and nets. Eyes wide with eagerness, they tilted their faces up towards the sky and for a moment all stood still and silent, ears tuned to the birdy voices peep-peeping above. But the sweet sound was torn apart by a roar of joy as the males became aware of the enormity of what they were witnessing: a mighty flock of birdybirds circling overhead. They raised their weapons and one by one began to chant the word, "Meat." They stamped the ground, clapped their hands and shouted into the air. Almost too loudly, for it nearly drowned out my soft singing. When I was sure that they were near to fever point, I switched my frequency.

The slavering males, blind to all but their own impending gratification, did not notice the increased size of the big-beaked things that began to descend, or the retreat of the smaller, edible ones. I pulled Wirt close to my side, waited until the sky was almost black with wings, and then gave forth a sound most pure in its intent. A note that caused the predatory birds to dive.

My mouth ran dry and I held onto Wirt with all my strength as raptor after raptor plunged into the gathered males. Their talons tore, their razor beaks slashed, and I swear I saw an ear or two come off. Despite attempts to fend off the resolute birds of prey with their sticks, the Nearlys and 'dults fell heavy under the weight of so many. I gave in to gloat at the sight of these big proud males, that only the night before saw fit to defile a gentle creature for their sick needs; squealing like a girlygig with a tangle in her hair.

I smirked as they lay huddled in one great lump of fear, all weeping like the yellow-bellied brutes that they were. Their hands were torn to shreds from paltry attempts at shielding their faces from the relentless strikes of owlets, buzzards, eagles and smaller raptors. Only Brennus remained standing, swishing his great cudgel this way and that, hitting nowt but air.

I watched as the ground became red with their blood and moved my feet away from its sticky flow. Wirt trembled and I gripped his wrist. He took in a shuddering breath and whispered into my ear, "I cannot bear to watch." I let him turn away and stood steady for a while longer.

How pitiful and shrill were the shrieks from these less-than-males. How satisfying to witness their downfall in all its glory. "Let us away from this scene of carnage," I said. Wirt nodded his head and headed towards the woods. I followed and amidst the cries and sobs, heard Brennus yell in defiance.

"Down some if ye can. We must salvage something from this horror. I promised ye all some meat and that is what we shall have."

I stopped, ready to return, ready to bring forth more if this fearless and foolish male believed that he could win, when a shaky voice cried forth, "Nay, wait! These are not birdybirds. These are hawks and bigger. We cannot eat this meat."

So right he was, for raptor meat like all other flesh from animals, is poison to all hominids alike. I let out a "Ha!" and spid-sped into the forest in search of Wirt.

CHAPTER 5
Encounter With Some Witchy Stuff

I caught up with Wirt secs later. He was bent over, hands on knees catching his breath. I tapped his shoulder and he jumped higher that a grasshopper avoiding a snakey's jaw and swooshed round to face me. He pulled me to his chest and I felt his heart beat fast. He held onto me with a strength I had not expected. His grip was so tight upon my clothes that it almost stopped my breathing.

I gasped in tiny lungfuls and said, "We must keep moving."

"Aye, we must."

"Relinquish my person a tad, so that I can gulp some air. At least enough to keep my feet clip-clopping fast."

"Sorry," he said and let go.

I straightened my crumpled tunic and we ran deeper into the woods. I halted 'bruptly when I came to what appeared to be a dead end. A large cluster of densely packed trees obstructed our progression. Wirt bumped into my back, and as one we fell to the ground. I lifted my face from the floor, sat back on my haunches and wiped the dirt from my eyes. Wirt stared at me with an expression of terror and buried his face into my knees.

"All clear, Wirt. We are in no danger," I said by way of soothing his anxiety. He did not budge and I had to prise and pull his stiff fingers away from my trousers. Which, because of his manhandling, were plucked quite shapeless.

"Birdies. Birdies. Big and nasty. They came before, when I was bub. The raptors butchered my lil' sis. Plucked her from my mams teat. How? How ye do this thing that brings them to yer bidding?"

Wirt put his head in his hands and rocked back and forth between soft sobs. I touched his shoulder tender-like and he stopped. He dropped his hands and gave me a fearful stare that made me feel ashamed somehow. I shrugged and simply said, "They named me well. I have talent for the voicing of things."

"Why didn't the birdybirds come too?"

"Their song is not the same. Took me more than it should to recognise the difference. Got the scars to prove it."

"This ye can do for everything?"

"Nope. Only things I can call are those that sing."

"Then we must trundle forth before the dark settles. Before the Wolfies come out to feed."

"Goodly plan, but to where? You know these parts?"

"Some. I came out beyond that wall of oaks and across the clearing. Walk it before moon up, mebbe less. But, cannot. Should not. I was sent to camp like all the teenbulls and must wait until I am Manlyman. Fems do not want us till then. Fems will be aggrieved on seeing my nondult face. But here there be Wolfies, as fierce as all them raptors in a bag. They have taken more bubs than all the Kiddiefilching Agros in the land."

"What do you know about those Peados?"

"Only what I hear."

"And what words did you take in?"

"They take the tenderest, sweet ones. Ones that have the Meekness."

"My bro-bro was biddable. Too much so."

"When was he taken?"

"Not more than eight days before I came to your camp."

"Then I hope he will be living. Safe if ye can find him"

"Where to look?"

"That I cannot say."

A crick-crack and snap sound ceased our conversation, and I adopted the guarding stance. There was another splinter break behind us, and another and another. Wirt ran to my rear and we stood back to back ready to attack. I only hoped that if it were Agros following us, that they would be small in number.

I whispered low, "You have the skill?"

"As good as any when not outnumbered."

"Good enough. Stay this close." He pressed his back against my spine and I yelled to who knows what. "Come out you milksops. Face us like a Backpacker S.A.N.T."

A snort of some magnitude greeted my blusterings, and I felt Wirt's body tense as stiff as a dead man's knee. "Wolfies." He hardly spoke the word before a huge one sprang at us from the thick greenness.

It landed by my feet. I stayed rigid as a tree trunk, hardly daring to breathe and wishing with all my might that I wore the same metaplasmonic material that my Synthbag was made from. Then I too would be rendered invisible by the light trick camouflage and able to run away undetected.

The animal lowered its neck, raised the thick brown-black fur along its back and thrust its head forward. Its thin lips spread wide to reveal deep red gums that held the whitest, sharpest teeth I had ever seen. I swear its drool dripping fangs were the size of my fingers. It gave forth a belly-rumbling growl and narrowed its amber eyes. Four more slavering creatures crept out, all with jaws wide open, all making noises of threat.

They pawed the ground and snorted hot air from flared nostrils and I thought myself gone deaf, so loud was the sound of my blood as it pounded in my ears. The snarling hounds moved nearer to our trembling selves, so close that I could smell their carrion flavoured breath. I felt Wirt's shoulders dig into mine and again he said the word "Wolfies."

As fearless as I am, and skirmish trained, I knew that we were outnumbered and soon to meet our doom. The beasts wrinkled their snouts, growled most fiercely and hunched themselves low, ready to strike. Too near to death to think straight I slowly raised my hand up and over my shoulder and delved into my Synthbag knowing not what I was looking for. I came upon the used sponge bag and an idea sparkled in my brain.

I cautiously pulled out said item, yanked the pouch apart, took out four bloated absorbs and threw them one by one into the shrubbery, saving an extra squishy swab to taunt the beasties with. I swung it round and round and they followed it with their ravenous gaze. Once I was sure that they had taken the bait, I threw it in the near direction of the others. The Wolfies sniffed and drooled a bit, then lurched into the denseness. For the first time since reaching readywomb, I was grateful for being afflicted with the heavies. We ran full pelt in the opposite direction, towards the barrier of trees and pushed our way through it.

Wirt slowed his racing legs when we came to a clearing. We stopped by an ancient gnarly tree trunk surrounded by tall yellow flowers.

"Wolfbane," Wirt said.

"This you are assure of? The pics I have seen when we did stuff about nature and the like in geog class, show a pretty blue petaled plant. Not this scraggy permutation."

"The blue stuff is not true. It goes by the name 'Monkshood' and although quite as deadly, it has not the power to inflict the extra hurt upon the Wolfies."

I reached to pluck some up to stash in my Synthbag for later use, but Wirt pulled my arm away.

"Do not. Even the tenderest tap will harm. Be not fearful. Wolfies will not follow us here."

"Truly? I had thought it a myth."

"No myth, all fact."

I rubbed a burgeoning welt on my arm that came from the briefest of contacts with the shrub and said, "Not sure I wish to traipse amongst such deadly veg."

"Worry not about harm. I know the way." He scrunched himself down upon the earth and scratched the ground looking for something under the surface.

He slid his fingers around a fibrous root, yanked it out and began to chew the end.

"If you are with hunger, Wirt, I have many a sachet of grub and the like," I said and took a pack of Soysausage from my bag. "We can mix it up, make a fire and eat heartily from its goodness." He shook his head and I stuffed the dried meal back from whence it came. He sat upon a rotting wood stump and held up the root.

"This protects. I make a paste of it and smooth it into my flesh, then all is shielded from the plants poison."

"My jaw drops at your wondrousness. Come, I will masticate too and make us both immune."

I rested myself beside the teen and chomped upon the rootlet, pursing my lips at its bitter taste. I spat out the pulp into my hand, and then rubbed it along my forearm, fingers and palm. He did the same. Then indicated by way of mimicking a kittle lapping at some cream, that he required some water to rinse away the excess mulch. I took a flask of said same wet and gargled-spat until my mouth felt right. Wirt followed suit and we set about procuring our armour against the Wolfies.

Wirt laid the plantlets on some giant leaves that he plucked from the undergrowth, and wrapped them up tight. Folding them so neat and cleverly that they did not require a binding to keep them from falling out. I stood and watched his dexterous manoeuvres and became aware of a warmth growing inside my gut, that wasn't all that displeasing.

"Amongst this magic plant, we can abide and have ourselves a sitting down," Wirt said.

"Most rightly, for I have a belly ache for lack of something good."

I kneeled and fumbled in my Synthbag for a pack of Soylygrub and some water. I pulled out one of my faves, Soymadras, and turned back to Wirt. He was nowhere to be seen.

"Wirt!" I yelled. No response. "Wirt!"

A sudden sickly feel crept up my spine. I dropped the food and ventured toward the woodier parts and called his name again. No answer. My breath came out quick and hot. I thought I heard a low growl somewhere near. I backed off and the noise became louder. I strained my eyeballs searching for signs of animal, but saw nowt except for tree.

The sound again.

It was close. So close that I thought it must be an invisible creature. There used to some back in the oldie days, when NotSoGreatBritAlbion was called the Youkay. When the sea was not dead, when creatures called squids abided there. They could change their colour to suit their environment using tinted liquid filled sacs inside their skin. When they squeezed their muscles, the cells grew bigger and the pigment spread out making them quite lost to sight. My class learning memories ended when something touched my shoulder. I spun round, fists at the ready. Wirt ducked just in time, for I sent forth a mighty left hook jab.

"Calmly Adara," Wirt said.

"You are safe?"

"That I am. Why ask?"

"Did you not hear the snarling creature?"

"I did not."

"Then listen with me."

We stood in silence and cocked our ears up wind. A mighty snarl burst though the quiet and Wirt chuckled.

"That was no animal sound."

"Than what?"

He poked my tum and it grumbled.

"It is ye. The source of noise, listen."

I did and heard my innards churn and complain most forcibly.

"Here, I come bearing nosh," he said and held out what looked like a mummified turd.

"What in huffin' hellfire is that?"

"Carrot. And this is Pignut, and these are 'shrooms," he said and proceeded to pull out a variety of dubious looking objects from his skirt pouch.

"These things we are to eat?"

"Cook firstly."

I picked up my Soylygrub and waved it underneath his nose.

"This is food, proper."

Wirt shook his head and squatted down next to the log we'd sat on to chew the magical root. I leant my bottom against it and watched Wirt drag together leaves and twiglets. He placed them on top of each other, forming a tower of dead foliage and branchlets. He took some flint and a piece of hemp string from his pouch and bent close to the mound. I ogled, fascinated as he scritch-scratched at the flat stone until a surge of sparkles danced around the ragged material. Then he blew as gentle as a sleeping bub, and I saw the tiny sparks ignite the hemp. A bright yellow flame and then another and another, tongued up the tower.

Wirt, created fire.

I kneeled beside him and grinned for all to hear as the flames jumped higher and higher, as he piled on more dry and dead-dead wood. With some twiglets and string he fashioned up a tripod and straddled it over the blaze. As quick as a spider knitting her web, he used his forefingers to knot together a pouch.

"Ye have a cup or bowl in that magic sack of yers?"

"Both," I said and handed him a nanosteel croc.

"Goodly. Water too and something to aid us in the eating of this meal?"

I gave him my flask and an all-in-one cutlery device that he opened to reveal a spoon, fork and small knife. He laid the utensil on the ground and put some liquid into the pot. Then, he filched out a ragged dagger from the holster on his skirt and chopped up the miscellaneous titbits. Wirt placed them in the pot and the pot in the knotted holder, and attached it to the twiggy stand.

"The taste may benefit from some dried 'erbs," he said as he took out a sachet from his skirt pouch and sprinkled it on top. I do believe I smelt the tastiest smell I have ever breathed in. I didn't have the sentiment to tell him that I had a firebox and that the Soylygrub self-cooks.

"Wirt, you are a sorcerer of greatness. Santy Breanna showed me how to make a fire once. Too bad I wasn't paying attention that day, for if pressed to summon up flames myself, I think I would flounder. Where did you school to learn all this?"

"Here and there around the forest place. That's what we do in Manlyman camp. The best foragers make the best hubbies."

"Then you will be sought after."

Wirt blushed and shook his head. "That path may fork too broadly."

I looked into his moocow eyes and knew the right in his sayings. I decided to change the subject and learn more about these rustic folk.

"Is it true you cannot cleanse until you become Manlymen?

"Tis rightly so. At first our wishy-washiness, and holding on to the old fear of the virus, was nearly our undoing. So we sought a way to toughen up and keep from coughs and colds and the like. This muckiness is a solemn thing, a test of spirit and vigour. I do not relish such a life though."

"That is plain to see."

"Do ye not wish for bond with Manlyman? As befits a fem of yer years?"

"Nah."

"Ye are not like any women-folk I have known."

"So they say. Most girlygigs in Cityplace just curl their hair and speak in bubchat. Wouldn't know how to kick down an opponent if their squishy lives depended on it. I'm glad no Manlyman wants me for a Missus. The thought of snuggling up with a whitewashed male in a hygenehome churning out bubbies till I shrivel, gives me the heebie-jeebies."

Wirt stared at me for a sec, and then lowered his head.

"Mebbe, one day some fitting male will cross yer path and ye will think on different terms."

"Nah, well…Nah," I said, picking up the all-in-one and dipping it into the mushy goodliness in the pot. I gulped down several mouthfuls of the stew, cleaned the spoon with some of the water and handed it to Wirt.

"Ta," he said and daintily chomped down the rest of the food. I noted that he took particular care in fully cleansing the implement when he had done using it. Rinsing then drying it on the heat of the fire. He gave me a smile as warm as the flames and I could not help but assume a similar grin. We stayed that way for longer than was necessary and when our eyes parted, the goodly heat had waned somewhat.

A lazy wind burrowed through us and we both shivered. Wirt stood and gathered some larger twiglets and more leaves. He threw them onto the dying embers and they soon caught alight. He sat next to me and our shoulders touched. We leaned closer to the inferno and I swear I could hear both our hearts thumping fast.

Wirt snuggled closer and said, "In time, I believe I would be glad to have a young 'un of my own."

"You would make the finest pa, Wirt."

"Ye think so?"

"I do and then some."

A high-pitched shriek ripped apart our sweet reverie and Wirt looked to the aboveness with a look of fear upon his face.

"Do ye believe the raptors devoured all at camp?"

"Doubtful. Maybe a few dropped, but the rest more as like merely came to injury that can be fixed."

"I worry that word will spread like mildew. We must race to somewhere safe."

"Your home?"

"Mebbe, mebbe not. They may have news of what took place."

"Surely your mam would want to see you?"

"Aye, mammy would. I think. Nay, she would, of course she would. Come, let us go home," Wirt said and stood.

I kicked soil over the fire and replaced the things Wirt used back into my Sythnbag. He sniffed the air and pointed ahead.

"This way. Keep close and do not stray."

"That I will not do," I said and followed.

CHAPTER 6
Women Folk

Wirt's pace was quick and I struggled to keep up. The twigs and bramble things that littered the floor seemed to conspire against my weakling legs and tugged and tripped me so much so, that I conceded defeat and sat down upon a softly bump. Wirt raced on ahead and I had to call to him to make him stop. He gave back an ear-piercing, "Shhhhhhhhh, will ye," and crunched back to where I sat.

"You go too fast. I am not used to this terrain so much as you. I am breathless and scratched from the effort," I said and rubbed my calf.

"Ye must keep up. It's not so far. I didn't take ye for a sissy."

"Sissy? Me? I'll have you know, merely Nearly, that I am this orbits Roughhouse Champ. I beat a trainee S.A.N.T. in the final. A male, trainee S.A.N.T. at that."

"Aye, ye are brave and tough when it suits, and I have never seen the like with the raptors, but now ye fade like a newbie bub."

I would have socked him one for sure, if it were not for the fact that he was right. I hung my head and snorted loudly, then rose to my feet. He, all hands on hips and pouty-pout, had a look of solemn, especially around the mouth. I simply said, "Lead on, again. I'll follow without complaint."

Wirt puffed out his cheeks and made a clicking sound with his tongue, then turned and marched ahead. I clopped behind stifling the "ouches" that formed in my mouth each time a thorn sliced at my leg or arm.

When we had tromped longer than I cared for, Wirt slowed and stopped by a circle of giant ferns. Odd, I thought, that such greenery would grow in such a uniform fashion when all about us were random clumps of verdure and saplings dotted here and there. Wirt bent down amidst the ferns and for a moment became invisible.

Then up he popped, a smile upon his face and he said, "We are here. These frondles mark the outer entrance. If there is trouble or the like, a red painted rock is left in the centre to warn of danger. I found no such stone. It would seem all is clear for our arrival."

"I am all eager to meet your family and friends."

"Aye, it is hoped they feel the same way about ye."

"Word cannot have spread so far yet. They may know nothing of what has occurred."

"Only one way to know for sure," he said and took my hand. Together we walked all slowly through the large leaves, squeezing our bodies through gaps in the trees until we came to an archway made from twisted branches and frondly leaves. A large lattice woven screen, that let through but a tiny hint of what was beyond it, blocked the entrance. A rhythmic thumping flittered to my ears. Then a high whistle hovered for a sec before forming into a lilting tune. Music. Basic for sure, but of such a purity of tone that I almost felt my legs begin to jig with the sound of it. I peered through a gap in the barrier and saw a vast clearing with small round huts made out of what looked like mud and straw.

Wirt pushed the screen away and my eyes widened at the scene of hustle and bustle. The source of the music came from a grey haired fem sat on a stump blowing through a wooden pipe. Two small 'uns knelt at her feet and slapped the front and rear of two large square wooden boxes. My guess was that they were hollow inside as the sound that came from them was deep and resonant. Folk wandered around the place doing this and that and I smiled at the sight of 'dults and bubs alike frolicking to the beat and laughing as if Agros and their brutishness were but a dream.

"Home. Stay close and let me do the talking."

I nodded my head, he let go my hand and we walked through the arch and into a hubbub of activity. So intent were they with their playing and dancing, that the Woodsfolk gave us not a glance as we trod warily into the camp.

I marvelled at how well constructed the buildings were. Sturdy huts formed a perimeter around a Homeoak in the centre of the space. It was dandier than the one at Nearly camp and twice as big. Now this was what I had expected from my looking at the vids. Coloured leaves and garlands of rainbow stained cloth hung around the massive, gnarled trunk. The entrance was adorned with wooden beads hanging from string that made a soothing clacking sound when moved. I wondered how I could hear such a quiet noise above the din of the music, and realised it had stopped.

A young 'un, grubby from romping in the dirt, pointed at us and shrieked, "Mammy! Mammy! It's our Wirt and a stumpy nymph."

I was not enamoured with being described as "stumpy," but the "nymph" tag pleased me and in response, I brushed a little moss from my pelt and loons. Wirt stiffened at the sight of two large women emerging from the Homeoak. Their hair was braided in strands from forehead to nape and hung down to their waists like dead millipedes. They wore green tunics with long sleeves rolled up to the elbow and their brown plaid skirts fell so close to the floor that each time they took a step, dust was scattered here and there.

They strode towards us leaving a string of curious kiddles and other fems behind them. I saw oldies of both sexes pick up bubs and sit them on their shoulder so that they could get a better glimpse of what was about to happen next. I thought it more than quaint that these folk let those with advancing years live amongst them.

Wirt took a deeply breath and said to the stouter of the pair, "Ye look bonnie as ever, mam."

"What ye doing here? What have ye done? And, who is she?"

I leaned close and whispered, "They do not know. Best to leave it like that for a time."

"What she bletherin' about? Speak or I'll take the Lochgelly to ye."

"The what?"

"This," she said and produced the meanest looking woven stick I had ever seen. "Ye well know how it feels eh, Wirt?"

Wirt bit his lip and the smaller woman, who had a scar above her left eye, said, "Aye, look at him, he quivers with the thought of it."

"He does indeed Meghan. Always was a Jessie as well ye know." She relaxed her grip on the cudgel and spat at Wirt's feet. "Ye relate what's what."

"We…we…came to see ye mam."

"Liar!" Wirt's mam said and held the club above her head. "Speak the truth laddie or by the Greenman himself, I'll beat it from ye."

Wirt shielded his face with his arms. The wounded-eyed fem bent down, picked up a large stone and flung it smack into his chest. Wirt staggered backwards and I held out my hands to keep him from falling. He coughed and righted himself, only to be smacked in the face by same fem.

"Ow," Wirt said and rubbed his reddened cheek. She raised her hand again, but I stopped it with mine. She sucked air between her teeth and pulled away.

"Ye are nowt but a blubbering babbie. And yer friend there, why she looks as soft as fresh snow."

"We'll see who's soft," I said and put up my fists. The two women put their hands on their hips and laughed.

"Do not test them. Ye do not know what they are capable of."

"That she don't," the smaller of the two said. "Shall I call Bemia to beat the truth from him?"

What mean and nasty fems were these? His own mam ready to see him thwacked, his own kin wanting only to hurt and ridicule one who had them done no harm. I now knew why Wirt had been so unsure of our coming here. There is an ancient saying, "out of the frying pan into the fire." Until this moment I had never really comprehended its meaning. I was about to admonish said fems and stand in front of Wirt to protect him from this Bemia thug, when to my astonishment and utter bemusement, Wirt grinned and embraced his mam.

"Ye are full of wit and daffiness, mammy."

She responded by hugging her son so close and hard that I saw his face turn red.

"Ah, my wee laddie, how I missed ye." She let him go and looked me up and down. "Did I scare ye lassie?"

"Well-"

"Ha! Good jest for sure. Come let us sit down and ye can tell me what is what," Wirt's mam said and we followed her, and the one she called Meghan, into the brightly decorated Homeoak.

Those that had stood and stared parted as we walked and I thought I heard someone say, "This can only mean trouble fer us all."

Meghan parted the beads and we stepped inside. There was a whole host of kiddles, fems and oldies, all busy with a task of some sort. Threading, beading, pounding roots and other stuffs I did not recognise. They were so busy that I became at once tired and in awe all at the same time. The interior resembled the Homeoak of the Nearly camp in all except for the beds. Here the walls were free from shelves and were adorned with coloured handpics depicting family scenes, and pretty good resemblances of flora and the like. All heads turned towards us as we stood by the entrance. Low murmurs spread like a wind gathering to form a storm. Wirt's mam held up her hand, and all fell quiet.

"Cease yer chatter, we have guests. Go back to yer work and do not bother us. Come let us settle and ye can relate all that has occurred. For I see in yer eyes, Wirt, there is much to tell."

She took Wirt's arm and we moved to a sitting area by the great fire and sat down behind a round piece of roughly cut wood that stood on four hefty timber legs. Wirt's mam put her elbows on the table and rested her head on her hands. I tried hard not to look at her smaller than small thumbs for fear she would notice and become irked by my tactlessness. Fortunately for me her attention lay with Wirt. She stared into his eyes, then sat back, a look of anxious spread across her large-jawed face. Wirt cast down his eyes and I saw droplets of wet splish-splash onto the rough surface.

"Something badly has gone down with ye."

She turned her steely gaze upon me and I felt as if she were digging her fingers into my very brainbits. I sat back and put my hands to my temples, but the pressure did not abate until I blabbed, "My name is Adara and I brought the raptors upon your menfolk." I clapped my hands over my mouth and stood.

"Ye did what?"

"She called the eagles and such like. It was horrible, mam."

"Sheesh yer squalin'. I have nowt to say to ye son," Wirt's mam gave me another penetrating look. I snapped my eyes shut and felt a heavy grip on my arm, "My name is Andswaru, ye know what that means?"

I scurried around my noggin for the meaning of her tag and said, "Answers. You get answers."

"Aye, I do. Blab girlie, ye have no choice."

I opened my lids and she relaxed her grip. Wirt wiped his face on his sleeve and Meghan folded her arms across her ample bazoomies, and then gave me a narrow eyed glare. I took a long breath and did indeed blab.

"Do you know what Wirt has to endure in that filthy place? I know, I was there. Manly men, Nearlymen, all cowards, brutes and…"

"No, Adara, no more," Wirt said and I stopped.

"So, ye brought them to punish the weak-assed males? Much damage done?"

I was surprised by the calm in her voice and even more surprised to see her and Meghan break out in a shoulder-shaking guffaw. I gave Wirt a look as if to say "What the huff?" and he looked back with an expression as curious as my own.

"Do not look so flummoxed. All the 'dults but Brennus was sent to that camp as a punishment for lazy ways and lack of duty to their wives."

"Aye 'tis true. Brennus, my hubbie, went to keep all in check. How fares he?"

"Well, I think. On the last lookly back before splitting the scene, he was in command of the situation as much as was possible."

Andswaru shook her head and went to Wirt. She touched his face with tenderness, then pursed her lips.

"Ye cannot stay here. First place they'll come a-lookin' for ye. Although we are hard enough, we are not so tough to withstand the vex of those ye have hurt. Our other menfolk are away at work on Agro fields just beyond our boundaries. They thought that offering their services would soothe them into relinquishing more supplies. We can only hope it does. Nae, ye must go. Wirt, when the time is fitting those who have wronged ye will know not the comfort of home when they return. That I promise ye son."

Wirt nodded his head and came over to where I stood. He took my hand and squeezed it gently and I smiled a soppy smile. Andswaru and Meghan wrapped their strong arms around us both and huggled until we coughed.

"Away with ye now before I change my mind. Ye know where to go?"

"Aye, mam."

"You do? Where?"

"To the Ladies. They have a liking for me remember? Once, when all were a-bed, they smuggled me out and took me to their dwelling. I spent many secs supping things lush."

"Son, ye are full of surprise for sure."

"That he is. So be it. To the Ladies we shall go. It has been an honour to meet Wirt's mam," I said and bowed. She placed a hand upon my crown and I felt a pull as if my grey stuff was being lifted from its proper place. Then all was calm again.

"She will be yer pal son. Stay with this lassie."

"I shall mam."

With those words we left the women-folk and ventured back into the forest.

CHAPTER 7
Deeper into the Forest

Wirt took us deeper into the scrub and shrub. Gigantic ferns and thick-stemmed brambles stretched before us like a huge green, unwelcoming mat. The ancient plants towered all around us, and if I did not know better, I would have thought us shrunk to the size of a beetle and cast into this world of giant foliage by the hand of a bub. I looked to the sky for some sense of space and light, but saw only a canopy of leaves that blocked out the light.

A thick mist rose from the moist ground and I pulled my Synthowool cape tight around my shoulders. The fog swirled around my legs and upwards until I could barely see in front of me. I peered into the haze and could just make out Wirt as he shoved his way through the clinging greenery. I took a tentative step but came to an abrupt halt. Something landed on my neck and bit down hard. I plucked off the squishy thing and flung it to the floor. I put my finger to the spot and felt a large round bulge. It prickled most violently and I scratched and scratched until I saw blood upon my hand. I took off my Synthbag, pulled out a Mediswab and held it against the wound until the cool took away the burning itch. I placed my bag back from whence it came, and hastened after the ever-diminishing figure of my friend.

A high-pitched buzzing sound filled my ears and I waved my hands around my head to disperse a cloud of near invisible gnats that billowed around it. Wirt was far ahead and I did not relish the notion of lingering amongst these bloodthirsty flies, so raced forward into the darkness swatting at anything that flew into my path.

"Wirt? Are you there? Wirt?"

"Aye. I'm here. Where are ye?"

"Right behind you, I hope," I said and stumbled again.

"Keep going straight ahead. I'll stop for a bit until ye reach me."

I picked up my feet and continued on, moving in exaggerated high-kneed steps so that I would not fall prey to the bits and bobs that lay in wait ready to topple me. The darkness persisted, making it near impossible to see my way. I halted and remembered that I had packed a source of artificial light. I reached down inside my leg coverings to the strapped on Brilite, pulled it out and was just about to press the switch when Wirt appeared from amidst the gloom. He stopped me from turning on said torch by grabbing my arm and shaking a finger at my face.

"We must proceed in stealthiness. The Ladies are sought after by many a Manlyman and Agro alike. If we are detected, they would surely do us harm. And I would not lead them to the Wenchstead. It is a hidden place and for good reason."

I acquiesced and put my torch away, though not without uneasiness. For I heard much cracking of branchlets, not broken by familiar feet.

"There are sounds that would indicate threat," I said.

"Do not take fright so quick. Most of what ye hear is but the snap and tumble of rotted branches falling to the ground and landing on stones and such like."

I gave him a stare suggesting disbelief.

"If Agro or kin were a-following us, they would not be so indiscreet as to allow our ears to discern their presence."

"Goodly point. Yet there is a tug in my belly that will not go."

"That is a sign of one who knows the ways of stealth. I think ye will make a fine S.A.N.T."

My Santy Breanna's face flashed through my mind and I recalled with pride her brave stance against the latest Agro onslaught at Cityplace. She was fierce and tough and gave them a taste of "we will not succumb to the likes of you." She sent them packing and no mistake. I felt a lump swell in the back of my throat and lowered my gaze.

"Ye look to the ground with a sad mouth. What gives, Adara?"

I sniffed and brought my eyes to meet Wirt's. He looked at me with a gentleness that Santy used to and I felt a tug of homesick.

"I have let my Santy down."

"How so?"

"I have veered from my mission to find my bro. My tum churns with the notion that the filthy Agros who took him will cause him suffering. That because of my lack of purpose, he will come to great harm."

Wirt touched my arm and the coldness in my chest and belly waned.

"Nay, Adara, ye have no reason for shame on this account. Ye were took just like your bro. Fret no more. We will find him when the threat to our safety has lessened."

His words were soothing to be sure and dispelled the morbid images that hung heavy in my head. I took courage from what he said and blinked away the tears that crept from my eyes.

"The darkness looms ever more, Wirt. I cannot see that much so as to grasp our given direction. And I fear that if not Agro or Woodsfolk, then wolfies may be a-following."

"No wolfies on this path."

"Why so sure?"

"Look," he said, bent down, plucked a flower from a low growing shrub, and held it up to my face.

"This is of a sight familiar?"

I peered at the green and yellow plant and sighed a relief-filled sigh.

"Wolfbane."

"As far as the eye can glimpse."

"Which is not far in this murky atmosphere."

"The Ladies planted it especial-like to keep the nasty fangy things away."

"Therefore we are all safe."

"From wolfies to be sure, but not from-"

"Manlymen or Agros."

"Is right. Do not look so forlorn. We are closer than a suckling on its mother's teat. Come."

"I would feel safer if I could take your hand, if you would allow it?"

"It is yers for as long ye need it," Wirt said and offered me his grubby mitt. I placed mine in his and he wrapped his fingers around all six of mine and thusly entwined, we made our way forward.

He moved smoothly through the scratchety foliage and uneven ground. I tromped beside him trying not to fall. When I did succumb to gravity pull and ended up upon my rump, Wirt offered me his back.

"I'll carry ye for a bit. Until the ground levels."

I gladly jumped up. "Hang on," he said and I wrapped my arms around his neck. He wobbled for a bit, then found his strength and stood tall. I marvelled at his newfound brawn and relaxed into the warmth of his shoulder blades. My movement caused him to loose footing and he tottered uncertain-like upon his feet.

"Maybe it would be best if you set me down."

"Nay."

"But-"

"Just hold on," he said and tried to take a step. I thought I heard him moan.

"You are yet well?"

"Aye." I heard him gasp and loosened my hold on his neck. He bent forward and I felt myself slide towards his bot.

"Maybe you should let me go?"

"Nay. I can manage," Wirt said, then his knees gave way and down we both went into the mud and mulch.

I had never tasted rotting leaves. I pulled the slimy things from my mouth and hoped I would never again have cause to swallow such pungent sludge. I spat out as much as I could, then ran my finger around the inside of my mouth. I turned to Wirt. He too was gauging bits of twig and moss from his gob. He looked at me, picked a wodge of something brown from my hair and grinned.

"Mebbe, ye can go the rest of the way on foot?"

"Goodly plan."

Wirt stood, shook himself so that all the nasty bugs and bleck fell off, and then offered me his hand. I took it and he pulled me up.

"Ready to continue?"

"That I am. I would be done with this wood, Wirt," I said and brushed away some maggoty things that clung to my ankles.

"Then follow me, but stay close."

Wirt strode off and I hurried after, taking care not to relive my recent encounter with the mushy earth. We trod on, pushing foliage and fern from our path until the forest thinned and we came to a small clearing. There were many dead trees lying in rows on the floor as if someone had hacked them down.

"Is this area used by your folk for logging purposes?"

"Nay, we are not allowed to take from these parts. The Ladies have domain."

"Of this forsaken landscape? They are most welcome to it. Those prone logs will be a chore to clamber. I confess to being more than weary as it is."

"Do not fret, Adara. We are close. The Ladies abode lies just beyond the seventh fallen tree directly ahead."

I opened my eyes wide to let in all the tiny light that shone and could just make out a vast wall of thick brambles and the like.

"Good it is not far, for I am soggy in parts I would rather not be."

"Take my hand then and let us tramp quick."

I did and we trod speedily to a great log. Wirt leapt onto said stump and hoisted me up beside him and so we went on climbing and jumping up and over fallen tree after fallen tree, until we came to the spiky hedge. It was high and deep and dense and full of knotted stems with long dagger-like spikes. I pricked my finger when I tried to put my hand through. Wirt shook his head and cocked his ear to towards the sky.

"What is it?"

"Ssshh. Do ye hear that?"

I listened and heard a scrunching noise. I put my hand to my mouth and held my breath. The sound again, only nearer. Wirt pulled me away from the brambles. A hoolet cried it's sadly song and I jumped. Wirt pressed a finger to my lips then pointed to the wall of thorn and spike. The hoolet cried again and Wirt cupped his hands, pressed both thumblings together and put his pursed up mouth against them. He blew and out came the best hoolet scream I'd heard issue from anything other than the birdie itself. He did it two times more and the veggie wall parted.

CHAPTER 8
All Cosy in the Wenchstead

A Lady dressed in a blue skirt and tunic with a shroud of lightest white cotton, stepped out from the underbrush and walked in our direction. A small, sly smile spread unperturbed across her well-washed face. She had long straight black hair with such a sheen that I swear if I were to look directly at it, I would see my own refection staring back. Her eyes where large, and almost as dark as her hair. And her skin was the colour of melted choc. There was not a wrinkle or blotch anywhere and I thought she was the most beautiful fem I had ever seen.

She took Wirt's hands in hers and twirled him round until he gasped for air. Then embraced him with as much affection as if he where her own big bub. Wirt pulled free and gestured towards myself. I limply waved and grinned a grin of mortification. Glad the dimness hid my deep red skin. She glanced me up and down and nodded her head. Then Wirt and me and she scrambled through the thicket wall and out into a bright-light clearing.

There were at least a dozen colourfully painted small log cabins all in a row, with a larger dwelling to the far corner opposite the entrance we came in by. All had roofs made from sun panels not unlike those we have in Cityplace. I was impressed that they owned such tech so far from the hub of civilisation. Round solar-powered lights attached to the outside walls of their abodes illuminated the quadrant, and shed such a soft glow that I thought I was watching a vid. There were traces of artistry too. Each front door had its own craftily crafted gold-like knocker in the shape of leaves. I turned my wonder-filled head this way and that and saw in the centre of the complex, raised soily beds full of flowers, veg and fruit bushes. Then to my further amazement and joyousness, a host of real live pets tumbling and jumping amidst the muck and dead leaves that swirled around our feet.

"You have bunnybuns and pupples and..!"

"And chikkles and kittlekits. But they are elsewhere."

I stared open-mouthed at the sight of animals that bore no trace of the usual Clonie defects or disease-ridden abnormalitics. When I had come across such beasties in vids or mags, they had a sorry appearance and were firmly from the past. To my knowledge, which is quite limited, no such creatures exist in thisdayandage. Yet here they were. I clasped both hands against my cheeks and blinked in disbelief.

The Lady chuckled, clapped twice and within a bubs gasp, other Ladies appeared from behind the closed doors. I had never seen such human perfection. These fems had none of the misshapenness that afflicts us paltry hominids. I stared down at my stumpy six fingered mitts, then at their slender five digited hands and felt quite roly-poly. Even Wirt, with his fine features and long leggy-legs had the Woodsfolk curse of shortthumbs.

"Ladies, Ladies all, come gather and welcome our dear friend Wirt and his somewhat sturdy companion. Who's name I do not know, and do not want to if she would rather not give it. My name, dear treasure, is Audrey."

Well named. A noble strength was present in her demeanour all rightly. I felt giddy surrounded by such comeliness and stuttered out my name expecting the usual cries of expectation. But no, not a thing occurred. Instead the divinely creaturelings embraced me one by one and uttered their own epithets.

"Well now, let us all to the meeting house and partake of refreshment together. Walk with me stranger and inform me of the threat you are most assuredly fleeing from."

Audrey entwined her arm in mine and I inhaled a whiff of her odour, an aroma that caused my nose to twitch with delight. It was as if I were surrounded by flowers, all in bloom. I breathed in her perfume and let Audrey guide me towards a large wooden house adorned with garlands of wolf bane. I turned my head to see Wirt all but drowned by a sea of waftly Ladies eager to caress his cheek and face. Such was the atmosphere of merry, that for the first time since leaving Cityplace, I actually felt at ease.

I waved to Wirt, but he was engrossed in chat with the Ladies and did not notice my gesture. So I dropped my hand and walked with Audrey to the meetinghouse. It was a jolly building to be sure, the colour of a summer sky and it had big red and white flowers painted here and there. We climbed the five wooden steps to the entrance and Audrey let go my arm. She opened the door, which boasted a huge gold knocker fashioned to resemble an oak leaf, and flicked her fingers in way of presenting the interior.

"Come in, come in and sit. Our dear Wirt will soon follow I'm sure," Audrey said and pointed at a host of finely patterned soft bags propped against the walls. I plonked myself upon a vastly sized pillow the colour of the rising sun, sank into its squishiness and let out a rightly sigh. I gazed around the room and saw such splendid chattels. There was a table as big as three Manlymen that near filled the entire space. Silver candlesticks ran the length of it and high-backed chairs with curly carved legs were pushed underneath and each had a plate and shiny cutlery set in front. A fireplace the size of three wolfies belched out roaring heat and a sweet pine-scented smoke. Before it, curled up quiet-like upon a red woven rug, lay a brindled kittlecat and its three kittles. Before this day I'd only ever observed said felines on my lapcom as vids or games. A red-haired Lady with big green eyes and freckled skin entered carrying a tray with two large mugs upon it. She gave said cups to Audrey, winked at me, bowed and left us alone.

"That was our dear Odelia. She is a prize to be cherished, as are all or dear friends." Audrey lifted her chin and scrutinised my face through half closed eyes. "You are from Cityplace are you not, my dear?" Audrey asked and handed me a cup of steaming wet. It smelt like sweeties, only better and I took a grateful sip.

"Choco-real and no mistake." I gushed. Then realised the rudeness at not answering her query and added. "Is right, I am a Citydweller. Or was."

"I wonder if you would tell my humble self, why you are here with little Wirt?" She sat next to me and brushed a lock of dirty hair from my somewhat mucky brow.

"I have no reason not to tell. The Agros took my bro-bro and a City guard gave me cause to believe that their trail wandered deep into these woods. He did not, however, give forth the info that a Clan of Nearlymen and Manlymen abided near with."

"Ah. No need to expound further. I saw the discolouration upon dear Wirt's features. At the hands of those hideous males?"

"More than once from Wirt's own mouth," I said.

The Lady turned her pretty hands into witch-claw clench.

"Do not fret," I said. "I delivered a sentence to fit the crime."

"What did you do, my dear?"

I opened my gob to answer, but caught sight of Wirt entering with the Ladies. He strode up to the table and said directly to Audrey, "She sang and sent the raptors upon them. We fled and left them bleeding."

"Oh dear, I fear that they will be out for retribution," Audrey said and took my hand. "You and Wirt are in great danger. Manlymen are known to be fierce when wronged, and you two have wronged them greatly. I am amazed, to be sure, that you made it this far without molestation. You must repose awhile with us, until we can be assured that the Manlymen have tired from the looking for you. Do not fear, we are hidden from all those whose company we do not wish to keep."

"Wirt found you out pretty quick."

"Ah, but only Wirt is privy to our whereabouts. He would not blab."

"Nay. I would not."

I chewed my lip and Audrey sensed that more was amiss. "I take it you have other concerns that weigh deep within?"

"Ever since I left Cityplace I have reason to believe that I was followed. Suspicion falls on Agros, since it was they who sent forces in to bend us to their will."

"The Agros have been busy my dear. Word has spread of their infractions concerning provision distribution. Even we Ladies have been caught up in their scheme. We sensed something ugly in their manner the last time we were called forth to entertain. Good for us that our reliance on these villains is minimal. We here have all but severed connections with them. Still, they have made us somewhat itchier than we like."

Her words caused a wave of high-pitched agreement from those present. I was glad in some measure to be talking of the far-reaching Agro threat. It seemed to dissipate its menace somewhat. And yet my innards twisted at the thought of irate Manlymen bent on our demise. I was all but given over to panic at the thought, when I felt a softliness swish around my lower legs. I looked down and saw a tiny kittle nudge and budge at my ankle. I had never felt such cosiness and I guess my face reflected said thought, for the Ladies all as one said, "Ahhh."

Audrey picked up the fluffy bundle and laid it upon my lap where it snuggled into my thighs. It turned and turned and made itself into a ball and for the first time in my life, I touched the furriness of a living animal. Oh, I had stepped upon beetles and buggles and the like, but I had never seen, let alone touched a breathing mammal. There were a few rigid stuffed ones in the class at the learning place, but they were old and musty and had eyes made out of glass. This, this was warm and soft and made a noise that made me want to smile. I did and let my hand fondle the tiny thing.

"It likes you. Not all kittles here would be so bold as to rest with a stranger. He knows you are no threat."

"It hums and vibrates so that it tickles," I said and all let loose a chortle. I heard a wailing cry and the kittle sat bolt upright. It opened its mouth and sent an ear piercing "Meeoooow!" back, then jumped off my lap and scampered towards what I believed to be its mam, who gave it an earnest licking before they wiggled-bottomed out of sight.

"How come you have such things? Are not all pets quite extinct?"

"That is what those in power would have you think. It keeps the order of things intact. As you can see, some animals survived and thrived, thanks to those who sought to preserve them for future generations."

"Such as?"

"The forgotten ones."

"And they are?"

"Moocow monks of the order of Maya," Odelia said.

I stared at these fine fems, my head all-full of what others had said about them. How they are foolish, vapid and only exist to ease the lustiness of males. But even in my short time amongst them, I realised they were as deep as the barren seas that surround our blighted land.

"I am grateful to said monks for their farsightedness in protecting such beasts. I do not think that I have ever been so overwhelmed by the caress of any creature before."

"You have a fine sensitivity about you, my dear, that is rare in these harsh times," Audrey said.

"Do not they consume flesh?"

"Yes. We feed them with prepared goo that comes from...Well, perhaps you will find out for yourself."

I was about to press the matter further when Odelia spoke, "Excuse me, if you will, but did I hear rightly that the young fem, Adara, called upon the raptors?"

"She did."

"Then she has the gift. She will be of use."

I huffin' well knew it. Didn't take long for someone to glean my importance. My mood of contemplation and cosiness left me quicker than a blink and I gave myself up to my full height, which was not so tall, and said, "Now look Ladies, I am more than grateful to you all for letting us abide here for a short while. But, I do not take pleasure in the ensnaring and ultimate demise of our birdybird friends. In fact I will leave now if you mean to force my acquiescence in that matter. In fact-"

"No, no. You misunderstand Odelia's remark, my dear one. Our prize egg layer has gone missing and it may be that with your powers you can persuade said chickle to return. Now calm down and resume your sitting position if you please."

"Apologies a thousand fold," I said and plonked my carcass back upon the softly pouch. "It's just that the last time anyone demanded my abilities be put to the test, well, hence the reason we are here."

"I have never understood those that partake of flesh. I find there are more than ample tit-bits to satisfy my deepest hunger, right here in the forest," Odelia said and sat next to me. "You have power for one so young."

"Not so certain I'd call what I do *power*."

Odelia smiled, slipped her arm around mine and leant her rust- haired head upon my shoulder. However, after not more than one quickly breathing in, did said head jerk itself away and a pretty little hand clasp its delicate little nose.

"Goodness how you throw up a stink. May I suggest a soak in something fragrant? Lest our finery become tainted."

"A thousand thanks for bringing my lack of clean to one-and-all's attention."

"Do not be offended. If you wish it, I would offer both you and Wirt the comfort and cleanliness of our bathhouse," Audrey said, and before I could say yes or no, Wirt clapped his hands and answered in the affirmative for us both. Audrey nodded to Odelia, who stood and proffered me her hand. I took it and she pulled me from my cosy place.

Wirt came a-scurrying over, linked his arm under Odelia's and mine and said, "Will ye find the chickle first?"

"I can but try. Although I have never sung to fowl before and am not certain that my call will be apt."

"Do not question your ability, Adara. Have faith in what you do and who you are and you will find the note that you require," Audrey said, and with her encouraging words, I left with Wirt and Odelia to call forth a chickle.

CHAPTER 9
The Chatter of Chickles

We stepped outside and walked towards the open courtyard that held the veggie beds and fruit bushes. I could not help but be gladdened by the lushness of my surroundings. Trees and ferns are all well and good, but they loom all haphazard and tangled like. Here all things green grew in such neat rows, that it caused a soothe to the eye and heart. Back home all I ever saw was concrete and stone. On special occasions some straggly plants were plopped into a dull container by way of brightening the place up a bit. All it did though was to accentuate the blandness of the place. Not so here. Here, all was leafiness and colour.

"I see you are admiring our crops, such as they are."

"I am indeed Odelia. They are a welcome sight and distract the thoughts to lighter themes."

"Really? And what insignificant subject are you thinking of now?"

"Oh, nowt in particular."

Odelia put her arm around my shoulder and drew me close. She reached out, grabbed Wirt's arm and pulled him beside her. We stared at each other and Odelia gave us a mischievous grin.

"I am wondering, Adara, do you have a beau where you reside?"

I pulled away and said all indignant like, "No I do not." Then I looked at Wirt and turned my back before my face caught alight.

"How sad. Still I am convinced such a lonely state can be fixed without resorting to a search far off. Eh, Wirt?"

Wirt coughed in an exaggerated manner and I felt certain my hot cheeks would set fire to something, so intensely did they burn.

"Come Adara, I but jest with you. Let us attend to the purpose in hand, that of retrieving our lost henyhen."

Her words soothed my abashment and when my skin cooled, I turned to my companions. Wirt rubbed his eyes and made the coughy noise again whilst Odelia lifted her shoulders and chuckled.

"So, Odelia," I said in as calm a voice as I was able. "I am familiar with the song of birdybirds and raptors, but I have never heard the sound a chickle makes. If you could perhaps give voice to resemble said noise, then maybe I can choose a suitable note."

"Oh, I do not need to do such a thing. Here, follow me and I shall take you both to the chickle coop where you can listen to their voices."

She walked a few steps ahead, turned and used her forefinger to beckon us on. I walked onwards and felt Wirt's breath upon my neck. Odelia linked arms with us both and we sauntered all-casual through the plant patches towards an area of shrubbery and flowers. We stopped in front of said flora and Odelia knelt down. She whistled faintly and I thought she had become addled. I'd heard of folk singing to plants and embracing trees, but I had never heard of whistling to bushes. I was about to say something along those lines, when I saw a movement in the undergrowth. A soft high-pitched whine followed and Odelia pursed her lips once more. There was a loud rustling and much shaking of leaves, then out jumped a snarling wolfie. I leaped up and backed away from its ferocious teeth and snarls. I called to Wirt and Odelia to do the same, but they just guffawed and took to rubbing the beast's ears.

"Come Adara, be not afraid. Look closer and you will see that this is not a wolfie, but a dowgie. Come, let it sniff your hand and become a pal," Odelia said and buried her face into the creature's furry neck.

I almost choked at the sight of a Lady making sport with a dreaded beast, and near fainted away when I saw Wirt bend low and let the thing wash his face with its tongue.

"Yeuk, in the extreme, Wirt. That wolfie's drool must smell vile."

"Nay, not so much. Come, it'll do the same to ye."

"Yes, Adara, please do make acquaintance with our dear Bliss. She is no beast, but a soft little dowgiewowgie. Aren't you my pet?" Odelia said and gave it a kiss upon the lips.

"Are ye afraid or something? Can ye not see the thing is no threat? Come, give her a pat at least."

I vowed to myself that although I would show courage and touch its head, I would under no circumstance allow the slavering creature to drool upon my person. I slow-stepped over to where they squatted. The fluffy hound gave a "ruff, huff" sound and I came over all a-feared.

"Do not cringe so. She is as tame as a that pebble under your foot."

"Eh, if you say so."

"Go on, stroke her head."

"Aye go on, Adara, she'll not bite."

I let my trembling hand hover above the pooch's head, closed my eyes and patted the rough fur on its head and neck. The thing gave out an explosive grunt and I pulled back my arm and stepped away. "There I have touched the thing. Shall we go to the chickle house now?"

"If that is what you want," Odelia said and stood. The bitch got up too. "You stay now Bliss, stay. Good girl." Bliss sat on her bottom and wagged her tail. To my relief she did not follow when we left her to continue our journey to the where the chikkles abided.

"The coop is not far, just around the back of the bathing house. Which you may use when we are done."

"Good, fine, let's get on then," I said and walked all fast-like to the building Odelia pointed at.

The unadorned hut stood at the far end of the courtyard, directly opposite the Meetinghouse. It was raised from the ground by four wooden struts, leaving quite a large space beneath. I tilted my head and peered into the dark gap to see if more dowgies were hiding, and to my relief saw nowt but blackness. We passed the front and went round the corner of the bathhouse to an enclosed rectangled area.

Metal posts no higher than my waist supported a thick mesh stretched between them that formed a cage-like structure. In the middle of the place was a long wooden box with a sloping roof, and all around that were a dozen small birdies with tiny wings and stumpy legs. I watched them dig their beaks into the earth and scritch-scratch the soil with their talons.

"Chickles," Odelia said. The birds raised their heads on seeing us enter and gave forth a low chuckling noise. That sounded as if they were telling jibes to each other and could not help but snicker at their own jollities.

"Do you eat these fowl?"

"Oh no. They are our companions. We only take the eggs they lay."

"I have never tasted real negginegs. Just the ones that come in powder form."

"The packet stuff has not a trace of egg in it, you know. It's made from corn flour, yeast and soya. I can assure you that the taste is nothing like that of real yolks."

"Do they cough them up?"

Odelia put her hand over her mouth to hide the grin that spread across her face at my dumb words. "No, they squeeze them out from their behind."

She bent down and plucked a hefty brown feathery thing from the ground. Odelia swivelled it around, put its head under her left arm and lifted up the rear of the bird. Then to my and no doubt Wirt's utter agahstness, she parted its plumage from around its bot and said, "Do you see that little opening?"

We nodded quickly lest she had a mind to poke the thing in our faces for a better look.

"When the chickle is about to lay, said tiny gap expands and out comes a nice big egg."

"What? Eggs get plopped out like… Plop?"

"Sort of," she said and carefully placed the bird back onto the floor. It ruffled its feathers, gave out an indignant "Buck, buck, buckaw," and then strutted off.

"As you saw, their seed, for want of a better word, escapes from a place not that dissimilar to your reddy opening. In fact their eggs are ejected much in the same way that all ripe fems ova are."

I touched my belly and wondered if chickles felt the same heavy pain that I did each month. I looked to Wirt and his face resembled a slowly rotting peach.

"Yeuk, in the extreme," he said. "Will ye cease describing in utter detail a subject that churns my tum?"

Odelia laughed and Wirt turned away from the chattering birdles. I stood for a sec and tuned my hearing to their sound. It was full of clicks and short sighs and was the cosiest noise I'd ever heard. The bird song I was more used to had an eager quality to it that smacked of fear and menace. But no such angst filtered through these creature's soft peeps.

Odelia knelt amongst them and beckoned to me to lower myself too. I did and remained quite still. After no more than a few secs, they came to me and set to scratching and clucking around my squatted form. I bent my head, closed my eyes and let their jabberings fill my brain. When I had listened to more than enough, I set to mimicking their chatter. The busy birds ceased their machinations and stared at me. I clucked again and they answered with a similar sound. After a few more attempts at communication, I sat back on my heels and in their own language, asked them to come right up to me.

Wirt opened his mouth wide and Odelia clapped her hands at the sight of chickles swarming towards me. They cluck-clucked all friendly like and stopped. I reached out and a small white one bent its head. I put my fingers against its neck and stroked. The thing made the sweetest little chuckle noise and I became quite lost in its gentle guttural clicks. Its plumage was so soft that I thought I'd put my hand into a cloud. It remained that way for a bit then raised its head, cocked it to one side and gave me a penetrating stare as if to say, "And what about our dear friend who's missing?"

I rose and looked to the sky. Then closed my eyes and focused on an image of a chickle. All went quiet. I took in a deeply breath and let out a "buckaw-buck-buck-buckaw" several times. Then faint and in the distance-like came a response not too dissimilar from the sound I made. I clucked again and the answer came back louder. The henlets became quite excited and joined me in calling until the air was filled with the sound of rapid "buck-buck-buck-buckaw." With a flurry of red-brown feathers, the missing chickle appeared above the hedgerow and landed with a soft thud at my feet.

Wirt and Odelia hugged each other and I stroked the silky downiness of the birdie. The other chicklets gathered around their pal and nudged and bumbed her until she flapped her stubby wings and strutted off to the far corner of the enclosure. The others trundled after her. I shook my head and sank to the floor. Three encounters with real-live animals in one day! I confess that I was overcome and let a tear stray down my cheek. Odelia fairly flew to my side and helped me up.

"Ah, so much to take in. So much you have learned and achieved."

I sighed and wiped my forehead. I noticed a creamy residue on my hand and wiped again.

"Euk and yack. Is that birdie plop?"

Wirt and Odelia nodded.

"I know what you need, a bath. All hot and steamy, and filled with scent. Many thankyou's for bringing our chickle home. We will all be forever in your debt. Come, to the bathhouse," Odelia said.

We took our leave of the birdies and made our way to the bathing house, which was but a few steps from the chikkie coop. We walked up eight steps and Odelia opened a rather plain black door. We went into the dark place and I wondered why there were no windows. Odelia lit some giant golden candles that were held in what looked like an overturned flower head that hung from the ceiling. They were goodly candles indeed and soon the room became a fiery glow. She closed the door and I turned my head this way and that marvelling at the splendour of the place.

In the middle of the red tiled floor was an extensive bath sunk deep into the ground, Ancient Roman style. Spiky black mats where placed around it to prevent tumbles from wet feet. The walls were all hung with multi-coloured tapestries depicting males and fems cavorting and the like. Some in so much detail, that I was forced to lower my gaze. I felt Wirt nudge me in the ribs.

"I have nowhere to look to avoid my eyes being flashed with pics of immodest acts," he said.

"That is not a worry to me as much as the fact that there is but one place to sploosh."

"Let there be no shyness between ourselves, for we are as like sisters all," Odelia said and twisted on a silver tap shaped like an eagle's outstretched wings. Steaming water flowed from out its spout and she took a green bottle from behind an arras and poured in the scented liquid.

"Come. Disrobe and plunge into the bath. I will bring absorbent cloth for you to dry your skin when finished. Go. Do not hesitate."

I stared at Wirt and he at me. Odelia giggled, shook her head then left us wondering where to fix our eyes. Wirt coughed and smiled.

"I have never seen a fem without her attire."

"And I have never ogled a male without his."

We looked to the floor then into each other's eyes and I felt a strangeness pull at my belows. I gulped and so did Wirt.

"Perhaps we can close our spyholes." I blabbed all-quick like.

"I like ye scheme. This we will do"

I shut my eyes and trusted Wirt to do the same. I took off my garments and heard Wirt's heavy skirt land upon the floor. I summoned up all of my pluck and stood straight.

"Take my hand Wirt," I said. He did and together we leapt into the hot and dreamy water.

CHAPTER 10
Mayhem in the Meeting House

The Ladies at the Meetinghouse thought us quite without reason when they heard of Wirt's blind ablutions and mine. Wirt gave such an entertaining account of our stumblings and bumpings that I found myself a-laughing with them instead of reddening at the memory. I reclined upon the comfy cushions and selected delectable edibles from a platter resting at my pampered feet. I peeled a boiled neggy and bit into its softness.

Wirt wrinkled his nose at my groans of delight and said, "How can ye chomp with such relish upon things that could be fertilised? It is as good as eating meat."

"Fear not, dear Wirt, we have no cocks to impregnate our girls. These eggs would go to waste if we did not partake of their goodliness."

"Will you not try one?"

"Nay, I'll not, Odelia."

"Come, Wirt, let me finish smoothing your nails then," she said and took his hand.

I wiped mine on a fine napkin and let another Lady seesaw my nails until they became all smooth. These Ladies had taken it upon themselves to treat Wirt and I to a preening and we both sat dressed in the softest cloth. I wore a pale yellow tunic decorated with hand sewn green petals and a crisp cream coloured wraparound that made the faintest crackling noise when I moved. Wirt was decked out in a maroon shirt and ankle length kilt that so enhanced his features that he looked more like a leader of Manlymen than an awkward teen. I caught his eye and as one we smiled a satisfied smile.

Three Ladies stood at the back of the room and played upon small stringed instruments. It was a mellow sound that added to our already relaxed state. Full to bloating on delicious fresh-fresh food, I almost forgot about my bro-bro and his plight. That was until a Lady I had not seen before entered. The sight of her roundness put me in mind of the first time I saw my mam all mumsly heavy with my sibling. The Lady shuffled straight over to Wirt, knelt before him and pressed his hands against her bulging tum. He closed his eyes, lowered his head then spoke.

"Ye will surely bring forth a girlybub. Her name will be, Devona, the protector."

I stared at Wirt as he delivered this portentous news to the wide bellied Lady. She embraced him fondly and all gave out a mighty cheer. He yawned and I quickly followed suit.

Audrey noticed and gestured for all to quieten. She stood and said, "The hour is very late my friends and I can see that darling Wirt is fatigued beyond tiredness. Ladies, to bed and escort our treasured Wirt to his place of rest."

Wirt left the hall all floppy against the preggy fem's shoulder and the other Ladies followed. I stood to leave but Audrey stayed me.

"I would speak more my dear, if you can bear it?"

"I can and will kind Lady. But first I must attend to the needs of my bursting bladder."

"Ah yes, my dear. You will find the rest room to the right of bathing hut. Here take this lamp; the dark is sweeping in fast. I promise not to keep you long from your slumber."

I thanked her, took the glass orb that contained a merry flame in some kind of ether, and walked out into the fresh night air. The stars were out again and I stood for a sec and watched them sparkle. All thoughts of my bro and his rescue, fading with every twinkle that caught my eye. A chickle chuckle brought me back to my senses and I hurried to the place where I could let go. It was a small hut with several cubicles and three bowls and jugs on stands, for the washing of hands no doubt. So much nicer than the Nearly camps efforts at ablution. I entered one of the small rooms and released all the wet that I had consumed. With a sigh I wiped myself on soft white tissues, washed my hands and meandered back to the Meeting place.

As I neared, I heard Audrey chatting with another in hushed tones. For reasons I am not sure of, I hid myself behind the entrance and listened.

"We must be cautious Odelia. Adara is in our charge now. The plan is opening before us and we must not waver."

"I know, but to hear of Wirt and his plight makes me wish to keep him here in safety."

"His path is with the Auger."

"He told me that her parents succumbed to a bug when visiting the Beyondness, and died from a contagion caught there."

"That does not ring true. Why would anyone, let alone a Citydweller, wish to go to such an inhospitable place? I wonder if it was not a tale told to a child to keep her from knowing some awful truth."

I put my hand over my mouth to prevent me shouting "What the huff are you trying to say?", and slowed my rapid breaths lest they heard me stifling a cry. I moved in close to the slatted door and put my eye against a small opening. I could just make out both Ladies sat opposite each other at the splendid table. Audrey leant forward and took Odelia's hands in hers.

"More Meeks are going missing. Adara searches for her little brother. Agros are plotting something foul to be sure. What do they want with these kiddles?"

"Well guesses flow from all. Some believe they are to be a sacrifice to help the Agros with their ailing crops. Some say they are to be nookyslaves for some Peado's pleasure. Whilst others theorise that… That they are eaten as meat."

Audrey dropped Odelia's hands and sat back into her chair. Her face took on a look of solemn and a feeling of anxious crept over me like maggots upon a dead thing.

"We do not know for sure what the Agros mean to do with them, but whatever it is, it will be to the cost of the rest of us. Some things I have learned from various males. Things I have come to not disbelieve, since the same info has been delivered from many different mouths. There is tell that the Agros have a purpose for said kiddles. A purpose that will benefit some more than others. Adara has much to achieve if she is to free her bro and the other Meeks."

I could control myself no longer. These two fine Ladies appeared to know more about my fate than I did. I let out an, "Embellish me with further info regarding my bro Deogol, or I"ll-"

"Come in, my dear; do not be offended by our talk. We have only your well-being at heart," Audrey said.

I stumbled in and Odelia took me gentle-like by the elbow and sat me down at the table. She took the lamp from my hand and rested it on the floor. I stared at the angry red flame, and felt my cheeks take on a similar glow.

"Deogol, that means 'secret' does it not?"

"Indeed it does, Audrey," I said, pulling my gaze away from the light and onto her smiling face. Odelia sat next to me and stroked my arm.

"Calm now sweet thing and let our dear Audrey speak with you."

I un-tensed my muscles a bit and let Odelia continue to massage my hands and wrist. Audrey narrowed her eyes and stared hard into mine.

"Did you never wonder why he was so called?"

"Mam said it was because she didn't know she was with him until he was nearly out."

"A charming answer," Audrey said, "but I believe she named him because she knew he was to be Meek."

"Highly possible since he possessed great meekness right from outing."

"He had the gift of Tech?"

"The what?"

"Did you not notice that ability in your bro?" Odelia asked and kneaded my flesh more forcibly.

"Well, yeah, I guess so. He could fix and make the comps do stuff I could not."

Odelia ceased her rubbings and both she and Audrey exchanged a look of all knowing.

"That is what they want. This new generation that has the ability to figure out the innards of these machines that grow ever dated and soon will become obsolete."

I scratched my noggin and tried to make sense of what Audrey said.

"Have they not Techs of their own?"

"Rumour has it, my dear, that they have left. And without those to do their bidding and provide all comfort, they must and indeed it would seem, have found an alternative."

I let what she said sink in fast. My tiny brain squirmed with all the info and I rubbed my eyes and shook my head in an attempt to make sense of it all. A churning in my innards caused me to gulp and fear more for my bro than I had done before.

"I caught Deogol yearning after an image of a place the Agros sent to his comp. They are goodly indeed at charm and deceit and may have such ways of persuading the Meeks to do their bidding."

"That is a possibility. If they do succeed and advance their tech to outstrip ours, then we are all in grave danger."

"How so?" I said.

Audrey closed her eyes, clasped her hands and put them underneath her chin. She took in a sigh, parted her fingers and looked at Odelia and myself.

"We have something they want."

"You Ladies do?"

"Not only us, Adara. All. You know what I mean I think?"

I was about to shake my head and declare that I did not, but then I remembered what the Agros prized more than anything else.

"They want our reserve of seeds."

Odelia bit her lip. The light from the lamp on the floor flickered and went out. Audrey tucked her hair behind her ears and sat back in her chair.

"Most likely. And if they do succeed in obtaining said grain, we are all as good as dead. I see why the Agros need the Meeks. To decipher the codes where the seeds are kept."

Now I knew nowt about the politics of my home. And if I am truthful, cared even less about the eyesore that was commonly known as the, seedhoardplace. But Audrey's words gave me cause for great concern.

I wiped my face and said, "Now it makes all sense that the Agros came to ransack Cityplace. And the Woodsfolk camp."

"Soon they will come for us."

I raised myself up and slapped the table hard.

"They must be stopped."

"You are not the only one to wish that," Audrey said.

"Who else?"

Audrey took a sigh and looked at her fingers. I sensed there was much she did not want to reveal.

Odelia tapped the table and from the look on her face I assumed she wished severely to blab.

"Who else?" I said again and stood. Odelia, unable to keep the words from leaping out of her mouth, spoke.

"Others with a like mind. Others that wish to remain obscure so that that they have a chance to save us from the ever domineering Agros and their supporters."

"Odelia, hush. Adara does not need to know such-"

"I believe she does," Odelia said and stood facing me. "The others, and there are many, are out there gaining Agro info by means of infiltration and observation."

"What? That does not sound like much of a plan," I said. "An attack upon all Agros would serve us better than that."

Audrey waved her hand to suggest Odelia and myself sit back down. We did and said Lady continued in a hushed voice.

"Sometimes stealth has more power than force."

"I know little of the ways of spying, good Lady. I am to be a Backpacker when of ready age. I know only fist and clobber. If I succeed in my mission then I will not have to wait the one last orbit before I reach eighteen and be welcomed as a S.A.N.T."

Audrey gave me a heartfelt grin and despite my rising anger, I could not help but let my mouth mimic hers. She took my hands in hers and gazed deep into my eyes.

"I am sure you will be successful my dear, but until that time, your path will take a darker turn."

"Eh? What do you mean?"

"The hour is late. I have kept you from repose long enough. Know that I do not keep info from you to annoy. Only, to protect.

"This I do believe," I said and was overcome with a vastly yawn.

"There now, I have kept you awake when you should be snuggled and soundly asleep. Come my dear and I will show you to a place of rest."

I stood, and then to my utmost startliness, fell to a heap upon the floor.

"Goodness, you are all to pieces from what has occurred. The day you described to me has been more than one lifetime's events," Audrey said.

"Here, let me assist you to the cushions, as I fear you will not make it through the door to another place," Odelia said, and I let her help me up and guide me to the squishy squares that I had been so comfy upon before. I laid my head down and that was that.

*

Everything vibrated. I lifted my sleep weary lids and saw Audrey standing over me, a look of deep concern about her face. She was lighting candles despite the approach of dawn and just when she had lit the last one, they all went out as a gust of wind from an opened door rushed into the room. Odelia ran in with a look of fearfulness upon her perfect countenance. Now quite, quite awake, I stood and rubbed the sleep gunk from my eyes.

"Audrey, voices, male, have been heard outside the wall. Voices and bangs that would infer a gathering of Manlymen, or worse."

"It would seem that you have been followed my dear. Pity. We must hide you."

"What? Nah, too risky, we should go," I said.

"Where to? We may be surrounded. No, you will stay in secret for a while. There is more I should discuss with you."

"If that is your wish I cannot say no," I said. "You have been the very kindest there could be."

"A pleasure, my dear, a pleasure."

Over Audrey's shoulder I saw Wirt enter. I waved to him and noticed his face was all sad and downcast. He was carrying our things. On closer inspection I observed that our clothes had been washed and that my Synthbag had been opened. There is a light upon the left strap that appears yellow when someone, not the owner, has had their mitts inside. I grabbed said sac from Wirt's tightly grip and surveyed the innermost parts of my bag.

"Do not concern yourself, Adara. I gave instructions for your Synthbag to be replenished of goodies in readiness for your eventual departure. Is everything in order?"

"And then some. How did you come about obtaining Fruitles? I have not seen said product for many an earth spin," I said and laid the newly-filled thing onto the ground before my feet.

"We have our contacts. Now we must whisk you away to a place of concealment before the threat outside becomes a danger within."

"How did they find us Audrey? Were our guests followed? Or has someone spilled the beans of our whereabouts when out delivering?" Odelia said.

"Unlikely. Are we not cautious beyond cautiousness?"

"We are, but-"

"Do not contemplate the notion that one of our Lady's has been indiscrete."

Odelia bowed her head and I saw a frown come and go on Audrey's brow. A loud explosion blasted outside and for a moment I could not hear. All fell to the ground and Lady after Lady came scurrying in. I crawled to where Wirt was crouching behind a large cushion, and took his hand. He pulled me close and I felt a tear or two drop upon my neck. Another whoosh-bang! And another. This time a window smashed to smithereens and Audrey stood.

"No time for fear and fright inside. We must whisk away our beloved things. You know the drill. Hide the animals and seedlings, then yourselves in the bunker under the bathhouse. Then, when all is quiet, return back here quicker than a whistle blow.

I watched the Ladies swish their way out of the Meetinghouse and met eyes with Audrey. She beckoned me to join her and I stood, dragging Wirt behind me like an unwilling bub at firstdayatlearningplace. Before we reached her, another thunderous bang shook the entire room. We staggered and fell to the ground, covering our heads with our arms, as bits of hard outside stuff landed upon our prostrate selves.

No sooner had the shaking stopped, than another whiz-bang explosion stirred up more dirt and rubble and sent it blasting throughout the space. I curled up small and felt Wirt press against my back. And through the fear and crashing noise, Audrey's soothing voice was heard.

"Be not too startled and fretful, my dear ones. Although these bombings seem quite harsh, they are but testers sent to flush us out in panic. We will stay our ground. These shocks are not meant to kill or maim. My guess is that our assailants are not Agro but Woodsfolk males, come for retribution. I am saddened that they have come so close to our haven."

I raised my head and through the dustiness saw Audrey wiping grime from one of the overturned candlesticks. She caught my stare and smiled.

"You see? No real damage done. Come, bring Wirt with you and let us abide underneath this rather staunch table until they that wage this pretend war have tired. Although near, they cannot know where the entrance is, otherwise they would surely have swarmed inside."

I got to my knees and uncurled Wirt from his ball-like position, and then with him grasped most firmly to my waist, crouched down under the table with Audrey. She embraced us both and there we stayed, hands over ears for what seemed like two lifetimes, until the bangs and crashes ceased.

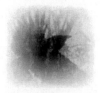

CHAPTER 11
More Questions than Answers

We waited long, listening for sounds of voices from outside. Shouts gruff and male came to our ears and I caught a note of deep frustration as bits of garbled words filtered in.

"Ye said ye knew… Wa? Cannae be here… They'd be out if they were… Right, try the next place." The mutterings and slashing noises faded and I let out a long sigh.

The sound of wood scraping on wood caused us to turn our attention to the door. It opened stiffly spreading dust and grit before it, and in walked Odelia, carrying two kittles in her hand, followed by the other Ladies. They slow-stepped behind her, with pets and foodstuffs held tightly in their arms.

Odelia walked to where we hid and said, "All noise and male stench has gone."

"As I hoped, they had no real clue as to where the entrance lay."

"I recognised a voice," Wirt said. "Sure it was Aiken."

"Aiken, that name resounds familiar."

"He is the one we no longer see fit to entertain," Odelia said.

We squiggled ourselves free from underneath the table and Audrey held out her arms. Odelia fell upon her chest and the kittles spilled onto the floor and sought out a hiding place behind a cushion.

"He is of a mean distemper and was the cause of severing all links with your tribe, Wirt."

"What did he do?"

"This, this is what he did, Adara," Odelia said and pulled up the sleeve on her left arm. I sucked in air and Wirt averted his eyes at the sight of a deep ragged scar that snaked its way around the whole of her upper arm. "I am no longer able to perform my duties. Males do not want a scarred Lady to give them massage and sweet words. It is only thanks to Audrey's kindness that I have a home to call my own."

"And always will my dear. Enough, we must put right what has been overturned. I would have you and Wirt come with me Adara. Odelia too. I wish to see for myself how far those males penetrated our defences."

We left the dishevelled Meeting place and went into the courtyard. Audrey shook her head at the sight of seedlings unearthed from their beds. She stooped down and pushed one or two back into the soil then sighed.

"There is much to fix and I have prickle upon my flesh from what has occurred."

"It is our fault. Nay, it is all mine. I was not cautious enough."

"I fear Wirt is right. It may be that we were followed. I did not think to cover our tracks, so swift was our departure from the Wirt's home camp."

"Do not blame yourselves. We are always on alert here. To be frank it was just a matter of time before someone sought us out. We have one or two enemies that would reap revenge for past deeds. Do not ask who or what, secrets are our most precious friends."

"Secrets seem to be all that I have to go on. The more I move the more I am bogged down by them."

"Dear Adara, do not lament so. Life itself is fragmented. Consider your plight a challenge to be overcome. Too much knowledge too soon can be a danger."

"How so?"

"What we don't know won't harm us."

"Eh?"

"An old saying, but an apt one. Come let us to the entrance and assess the damage done."

We walked to the place Wirt and myself entered. Odelia went on ahead and probed the bushiness with her foot. Audrey set to parting the greenery and squeezed through the gap we came through. Wirt bit his fingernail and turned away. I saw his shoulders gently shake and a surge of compassion washed inside of me at the sight of his distraughtness. I shook off my gloom and slapped him heartily across the back.

"Come, Wirt, time for blame and guiltiness is past. What is done is done and we must continue on."

"Aye, ye say right. But I have such a liking for the Ladies that I cannot forgive myself for causing such havoc."

"You are not alone in that blame. Let us do what we can to help."

"Aye, we at least can do that."

He smiled at me and took a sigh to clear his doom-laden thoughts. Audrey emerged with pobbles of stuff attached to her tunic. Odelia picked them off as she walked towards us.

"Panic, most severely over my dears. The entrance is intact. They had no clue."

"I heard Aiken say they were to another place. You have more homes?"

"Dotted here and there. We are cautious."

"What if they find one of them?"

"Then they will think themselves the victors at having caused us to leave. Look not so sad, dearest Wirt, all is now well and as before."

"Except that we should go," I said.

"Ah, yes, you must. Although it grieves me to be parted from you when we have just met. I have a liking for you, 'bird catcher.'"

I felt a modest lump gather in my throat and pressed the fingers she put into my hand with affection. Odelia linked arms with Wirt and said, "We must gather your belongings and make up a picnic of tasties to fortify your travels."

"Good, Odelia, take young Wirt with you. I would have one or two more words with Adara." They left and Audrey took my arm. "We will walk slow to the place I must now show you," she said and pointed to the far end of the courtyard. "The blue building to the right of the Bathhouse is where we must go."

I began to walk towards said building when Audrey stopped me by pressing her hand firmly against my chest.

"I will advise you on one thing only, be not trustful of those that seem above trust. Take no one as you find them and listen to your judgement, whether or not it seems appropriate."

"That was more like three bits of advice," I said and we smirked.

Odelia, Wirt and several of the Ladies approached from the Meetinghouse carrying my Synthbag and another pouch bulging with goodies. I took my special sack from the hand of the childcarrying one and hoisted it over my shoulder. It felt good and right nestled between my shoulder blades again. Wirt held the kittle that I had fondled the day before and I took it from him. I raised the furry thing to my face and breathed in its perfume smell and listened for the last time to its juddery purr.

"Let the goodbyes be swift lest we are all overcome," Audrey said and one by one Wirt and myself embraced the Ladies all. I handed the sweet kittle back to Odelia and turned to Audrey.

"Time to go."

"Indeed. Come my dears," Audrey said and led us to the cabin at the farthest end of the courtyard. The Ladies called after us to have a safe and successful journey and just for a moment, I wished that I did not have to leave.

We stopped at the entrance to the small hut, Audrey opened the door and we went inside. To my amazement, and Wirt's, it was not a room at all but a communications station. Shelves jutted out of all four walls and upon them were comps and phone portals.

In the middle on top of a large metal table stood a huge telescreen with images of an unfamiliar place. Wirt let out a tiny yelp and I confess to a slight gasp myself. I had never seen so much tech before, not even in the great library in Cityplace.

"Ye can see into that territory?"

"Yes Wirt, we can."

"Is that the Beyondness?"

"It is."

"Can you see more? Can ye see our camps?"

"No Wirt. Just the edge of that forsaken land."

I leaned close to the screen and felt Wirt's hand on my shoulder as he peered over it to peruse the scene before us. The image was fuzzy and all I could make out was a flat and dusty terrain. Audrey fiddled with a knobby thing at the side, and the picture cleared a bit. There was nowt much there that I could see except for broken and discarded lumps of metal. I turned to face Wirt. He shook his head and stepped back.

"Why can ye not see other places?"

"Secrets, Wirt, our lives depend upon them."

"How come ye have all of this?"

"This is not the time for explanations. Just know that we Ladies are more than we appear. Males do not look beyond the surface. That is our defence; the onetrackmindness of men. They believe us to be what they want us to be. Not what we truly are. Remember that Adara."

"I will and assure you that I understand."

"I believe you do. I believe below your surface many an intrigue and power lurks."

"Nah, just a need to find my bro."

"Where are all the trees?" Wirt said and stared deeply into the screen.

"The Beyondness does not have so much in the way of greenery, Wirt my dear. You may find it hard to take in at first."

"I do not like it."

"No, I daresay you do not, however, it is the place you are to go," Audrey said and tapped some wordly stuff onto a button pad underneath. The image zoomed in to show a host of strange, straggly plants and a relentlessly scarred landscape. Wirt turned to me with a look of disquiet and hung his head. Audrey noticed his sadness, reached up to a high shelf and pulled something down. She took Wirt's hand and pressed a red scroll into it.

"Do not look so afraid, dear Wirt. The Beyondness is not to be as feared as you might think. Like our camouflage it too masks a deeper quality that can be found with the right direction," she said and pointed at the scroll.

Wirt unwound it and grinned. "A map, Adara."

"A map to help you through the Beyondness. A place you will have to go-"

"To find my bro-bro and the others?"

"So it would seem."

"Do you know where they are held?"

"I have limited info; all I can do is what I am doing. The rest is up to you."

"Right, now I am afraid."

"Do not be. Know that you will not be alone in your search."

"Will I glean an answer if I ask what the huff you mean?"

"No."

We all smiled and Audrey simply said, "Perhaps you will meet some informed hominids on your travels and they may well enlighten you as to your bro-bro's whereabouts. It could be that a Backpacker may cross your path and have something to disclose."

"You tell without saying."

Audrey tapped the side of her delicious nose and drew our attention to the screen.

"You see that narrow path?"

We bended closer to observe. I squinted but still could not discern the track. Wirt rubbed his eyes and said, "There. It is to the left of that burnt out vintagecarthingy. Do ye not see, Adara?"

"Readily I do, Wirt. Is that the path we must tread?"

"Indeed so. Goodly fortune and may the Greenman or Babychesus, or Onetruegod, or whomever you believe in, guide and protect you on your journey."

I hugged Audrey and she held me tighter than I thought she was able. Then Wirt, tears a gleaming in both eyes, kissed said Lady on both cheeks. Audrey dabbed away his wetness and led us out of the hut and behind it, to an area of much greenness. Audrey sniffed the air and took my hand.

"Now, you must go on with your journey."

She directed the statement at Wirt. His face crumpled and he took a deep breath.

"Be brave, Wirt, and be as worthy as your name," Audrey said and embraced him most fondly.

"I shall be all ye expect and more."

"We shall all partake of grub again. This I know," I said and took Wirt's hand.

"Your company will be my strength."

"And ye my inspiration."

"No more farewells and sad bye-byes. You two have fate to deal with," Audrey said and pointed towards a gigantic patch of wolf bane.

"Push your way through there and into a low place that will lead you to the path I showed. Now go."

I swallowed hard, nodded my head and pulled Wirt with me through the dense green leaves.

CHAPTER 12
A Strange Encounter in the Beyondness

We emerged into what can only be described as a tunnel made from intertwined twigs and moss. The light faded abrupt-like and we were forced to crawl underneath the low canopy above our heads. Neither of us spoke as we hand-to-kneed it further through the leafy passage. I felt something snag at my gorgeous skirt. I stopped briefly and tugged the material away from a twiglet and heard it rip.

"Nay, ye have torn yer nice new frock."

"That I have. I did not think to change my dress from the night before, what with all the bangings and crashings, and the like."

"Good job Odelia made me wear my outdoor skirt and tunic."

"Yes, good for you. Shall we continue?"

"Aye."

I put my finger in the ragged hole below my knee and heaved a heavy sigh. Then shook my head in vexation at my foolish girlygigness and moved swiftly on. There did not seem to be an end to this tunnel and all I could see ahead was more of the same.

"Are we there yet?" Wirt called to me.

"No, and do not bother me with same question again."

We crawled on and every now and then I heard Wirt cuss as he too came across a spiky thing in the ground that poked and scratched. After more secs than I cared to count, I became aware that the air around us changed. Instead of smells of greenliness there came a pong of something not quite decomposed. The air felt heavier and so did my mood, which became lighter when the tunnel did too. I was able to see that the end was but a few bits away.

"Wirt, we are all but done with this dreary passageway."

"Good, for I am done with bits of stuff going who knows where about my person."

I stopped and leant back onto my ankles and Wirt sat next me. We looked out of a circle of leaves, onto a vastness of bleak. No luscious greenliness, or even a tootle-hoot of owlets to soothe our hungry ears. All around lay rusty clumps of twisted metal and black shredded round wheel like things. We stepped into the strange landscape and I looked up at the sky to make sure that we hadn't stumbled into some kind of Quantum flux paradox. But it was the same blue going on black.

The daylight was fading quickly. I turned to Wirt. He had his hand across his mouth and I swear his eyes were bigger than a moocow frightened by a carnie with a knife. I doubt he'd ever seen anything like the Beyondness before and was feeling all scared and wanting to run back to the Ladies. I confess I was somewhat fearful myself. I'd only seen it on the screen and the bits of junk that appeared random and small looked huge and forbidding in the half-light.

In the gathering gloom the trashed remains of automotomobiles and ribboned tyres took on a strange menacing form. I swear when I moved my head I saw a wheel move. I blinked and it became still again. The burnt out shells of what were once some kind of transport vehicles lay piled about, abandoned and rusted. Some were upside down and some were on their sides, doors hanging open like dislocated jaws dropped in disbelief at the sight of such wreckage. Now that I was standing right in the middle of this out-of-bounds realm, I came to understand how my ma and pa would have succumbed to the fatal disease they caught from their brief visit. Then I remembered what Audrey said; that the tale of their demise could be a fib. I became more a-feared and stood closer to Wirt.

"This is not a goodly place. This is a place of misfortune and grief," Wirt said and turned to me. I shrugged my shoulders and attempted a smile, but Wirt just shook his head and partook of a fathomless sigh.

"We should search for shelter as quick as quick. Night is approaching and who knows what kind of Clonie beast pid-pads around in the darkness."

Wirt hugged the scroll to his chest and I put my arm around his slender shoulders.

"Unfurl the map, Wirt. Let us see where we must tramp."

"The light is too dim, I cannot make anything out."

I took off my Synthbag and pulled out a small lightbeam.

"I have forgot how resourceful ye are. That pouch of yers is beyond any tech we have in the woods."

"One of the few things that makes our living that much better," I said, switched on the torch and shone it directly onto the map. Which in truth was little more than a sheet of paper with dots and dashes and kiddle-like scrawls upon it, rather than a geographical semblance of the place. I leant closer to the thing and Wirt traced his finger along and down the page.

"I am not S.A.N.T. trained, Adara, and find these swirls and lines nowt more than a jumble. I cannot make them out," he said and smacked the map with the back of his hand.

I grabbed the thing before it fell to the ground, put it close to my face and moved the light across it. I peered at the symbols and then at the sterile landscape before us and turned to Wirt. I held up the chart and he stretched out his neck to better see what I was pointing at.

"The massive X where my digit is shows our present location. The blobs and scribbles, I assume, are the broken cars and stuff we see about us. So, it must be that the straight black lines represent the path, or this stuff made from all things dead that sits beneath our feet."

Wirt looked down and scraped his foot along the ground. Plumes of ash-like dirt billowed up around us clinging to our faces and hands. It felt all greasy and we cleaned the filthy stuff off on a wipe I pulled from my bag. I glanced once more at the objects on the map and tried my utmost to glean their purpose. At the far end of the thick black line was an exclamation mark. The place we should head to no doubt. However, the scary outlines that dotted either side caused a lump to form in the back of my throat. I coughed and squinted into the darkening sky. Wirt licked his finger and held it up.

"Are you trying to discover from whence this sickly wind does come?"

"Aye."

"For what purpose?"

"Too keep in the midst of it so that our scent will be mingled. If any wolfies or worse are out here, we will need as much protection as we can muster."

Wirt put his palms against his forehead and closed his eyes. He remained in said state for longer than was natural.

"Wirt? Are you sleeping?" He said nowt. "Answer forthwith or I shall be forced to prod your bod."

"Sssshhhh."

"Do not make that hissy sound at me."

"Ahh, Adara." Wirt dropped his hands and opened his eyes. "Ye are not used to the outsideness to be sure," he said and fell to the ground. "Much can be kenned from smelling yer way."

"Erhm, Wirt? This dirty dustiness will surely clog your membranes if you choose to snort it up."

"I am not sniffing, Adara. I am absorbing through my nasal skin the scents of danger. Which, to a trained snout such as mine, will be as clear as a raindrop on a blade of grass."

I watched him bend his head close to the ground and turned mine in the direction of the oddly noise that wafted towards my ears. "Wirt," I said.

"Hush, I am all a concentrating and find yer outbursts a distraction."

"But, Wirt-"

"Hush, Adara. This is something I do well."

"No doubt."

"Sshhhh!"

"It's just that-"

"Quiet, fer Mother Nature's sake."

"We have company."

"Wha?" he said and stood 'bruptly.

I shone my torch ahead into what was now full on dark, and before our open wide eyes stood a creature of substantial strangeness. Human, no doubt, but attired in the oddest way. Its head was utterly obscured with a black helmet that covered its ears and the back of its neck. The face hidden behind a thin grey veil with an eyelet slit so the thing could see its way around. On the arms and torso, a heavy metallic pelt, woven into a diamond shaped pattern that looked hard to puncture. Thick black bands were wound round arms and legs, holding tech like things within. I'd seen such an outfit before. In fact, many times, and held out my hand to the stranger who was not so strange after all. Wirt inched his way behind my back and I felt his hand grab onto my belt

"Greetings," I said. "My name is-"

"Adara. I know."

I pulled Wirt from his place of relative safety. "This is Wirt. Or did you know that too?"

"I did. I am Eadgard."

"And are you lucky?" I said. He removed his veil and I noticed that his skin was much the same colour as Audrey's, but his eyes darker and rounder. He took my hand and shook it energetically.

"Only when I have my spear."

Wirt push me to one side and whispered, "Why do ye speak so familiar like this thing? Ye have a past with him?"

"I know him not. But his kind I am familiar with."

"And what kind is that?"

"He is a Backpacker."

"Special Army of the New Territories, Guardian faction," Eadgard said.

"A real life S.A.N.T. Ye are all that I expected and more."

"No doubt sent by our gracious Lady to give us much needed aid," I whispered to Wirt in order to salvage some ease.

"And how could she have done that?"

"I don't know."

"Ye talk has no sense to it," Wirt said and stared at Eadgard, who waved us towards him with an urgent hand gesture.

"Quickly, come with me. The night has come upon us fast. From someone who knows this place, I urge you to follow me to safer climes. Speaking of which, please turn off your light."

I did so and replaced it inside my bag. I pushed a rigid Wirt and he stumbled forward. I grabbed his skirt belt and he tugged it back from my steadying hand.

"I hope ye know what ye is doing," he said and I simply shrugged.

"You must keep close to me at all times," the newcomer said. "Do not stray. Do not wander off to relieve yourselves. If you must, then we all go together and keep watch. There are things here that cannot be seen, but can be felt and not always at the time. Do you understand?"

"All but the last part," I said.

"Venom of sorts. At least we think that's what it is. A creature invisible that either burrows into our flesh at a rate so quick we cannot stop it. Or, a thing that latches itself onto our parts and strikes when least we expect. Either way, it leaves us dead or wishing that we were."

"I think I'll be waiting for a place of greater safety before I release," Wirt said and gripped my shoulder.

Eadgard walked to where Wirt and I stood. He reached out and touched the sleeve of my dress, then shook his head and stepped back.

"Adara, your dress is far from suited to this terrain. Do you have other garments?"

I looked down at my torn and flimsy frock. The small holes and rips obtained from clambering along the tunnel had become larger. In places there was more flesh than fabric on view. I tried to pull together a vast rip that let my thigh through, but failed.

"I do indeed have more suitable attire."

"Good. When we are at a safer place, you must change your garb to something more fitting."

"That I will gladly do, for in this flimsiness I do feel more at risk than I should."

As if to rub said vulnerability in, a low deep growl grew from out of the unnerving darkness. I looked down at my stomach and waited to see if the noise was just an empty tummy grumble. It was not. For, the growl became a snarl of such magnitude that I near jumped with fright. Wirt let out an "Eh? Wha was that?" and almost drew blood so tightly did he force his fingers into my skin. The growl again, joined by another.

"Wolfies?" I said.

"Yes no doubt. But not as you know them. Bigger, hungrier and faster than those once-owned you will be familiar with. Out here are strewn the outcast Clonies of every type of creature."

I held my breath and felt Wirt press himself closer into my side. I saw the shadowy shape of Eadgard move nearer and I was grateful that he came to stand next to us, for I could think of no other more suited to saving our lives, if it came to that. The snarls continued, gaining in volume with every sec that passed.

We stood in the dark not able even to see our own limbs if we were to lift them to our faces. I turned my head skywards and saw nowt, no moon and no stars. I heard Wirt take a gulp and I too felt a dryness creep up my throat. I remembered the last encounter with wolfies had been in daylight and with some sort of diversion for us to make our escape. Out here in pitchy blackness, I feared for us all and shuffled nearer to Eadgard.

"Shhh! Quickly stand back to back in a circle and do not move, or make a sound. Do not turn on a torch or any source of light. The darkness now is our only protector. These hounds, although fierce to be sure, are about as bright as a black hole and will only attack when they see movement. Again I urge you to be as still as still and quiet as quiet. Now let me feel your hands," Eadgard said and Wirt and I did what we were told.

The grumbling, rumbling noise grew louder and I smelled a pungent wetness waft across my face. The darkness seemed to thicken around us and I saw red dots appear here and there. They winked and burned and I knew they were the soulless eyes of the Cloniewolves that Eadgard had described. A dagger like voice slashed into our ears.

"Heel! Heel, you rawbone jackals. Heel!"

A whip crack sound echoed round us and the burning flecks disappeared. I felt both Wirt's and Eadgard's hands relax in mine. A different smell spiralled up towards my nasal passages. A sweet and sickly aroma like something gone rotten.

"Strangers here, we tell. We leave all to mercy of houndlings, have ourselves goodly feed. Meat scarce to come by, we here not particular where it comes from. All better when fresh."

"Quiet, Marcellus. Stand back, shine our light."

"But Orsin-"

"Do as we say. Or Vea will hear of this."

The stinky pong diminished and I heard a sparkly crackle sound. Then a light as bright as two suns, or so it seemed in the blackness of our surrounding, splashed before our eyes. I held my hand across my face and blinked until my vision made sense of such illumination. I gave out a greatly gasp and let instinct propel me backwards at the sight that came into view.

A group of four human-like things stood before us. At least half a meter taller and wider round the shoulders. They wore half masks on their faces, coloured red with a fake hooked nose that resembled that of a beak from a hawk. Only their mouths were visible and they too were stained red. They were dressed in tattered furry pelts held together by what looked like giant teeth and carried huge black whips in their claw like mitts. The fire stick, that the one

called Marcellus clutched, spitter-spattered out
tongues of sulphurous flames that landed on the
ground and continued to burn around our feet.

"One we recognise. We sniffed this one before.
Quiet, noharm type, keeps to safe parts. These two
smalluns. These we not know."

"Orsin, grab them, make them squeal," a larger
than the other two things said. It held out its long
nailed hands and made a motion as if it were tearing
at our flesh. Wirt pressed himself against my arm and
I did the same to Eadgard, who was not a-quivering at
all. The one called Orsin made a hiss whistle through
his large white teeth and out lurched three of the
meanest looking wolfies I had ever seen. Their heads
where huge and framed with a brown matted mane
that extended down their necks. Each one showed us
their mighty fangs before crouching ready to pounce.

"Halt," Eadgard said and stepped forward. To my
surprise and relief, they did. "My friends and I are not
here to harm or injure. Merely to make our way
through your domain as quickly as we are able,"
Eadgard said and spread wide his arms in a gesture of
compliance.

"Only those with purpose tramp through
Beyondess. We thinking thoughts that you may be
conspiring with Agros," Orsin said and cracked his
massive whip.

"Never. I'd split my head in two rather than
collude with those cold-hearted tricksters," Wirt said
and clenched his fists. I hadn't expected such bluster
from this delicate male. His voice went all a-savage
as he continued his tirade on the farming guild.

"Those lessthanmen are to blame for all our woes
and grief. They keep honest folk afeard with chat of

looming famine and give us only dregs. Barely enough to keep us well. Then they take our strongest men and turn them into drudges. Nay to mention what they'd do if we did nay comply with their-"

"Enough! You speak and chittle-chat more than a fem in moon pull," Orsin said and the other two began to giggle gaggle and stomp their great feet. The ground shook from their efforts and I almost lost my balance. Wirt folded his arms and stood as tall as he was able. I swelled with pride as if a bubs of my own had won first prize in a wrestle contest.

"You distract with talk, lissom male. We turn instead to this prime fem and sniff out truth like dog in heat."

"You'll do no such thing, you lumbering lug," I said and adopted the stance of readiness in order to do battle. Big as he was, I was not going to allow this freakish creature to lay a nose or anything else on my bod. Orsin lurched towards me with a look of hate as intense as any I have seen on a 'dult, but just before he could grab, Eadgard stepped between us.

"No more of this. As I explained before, we are not your enemy. This young fem and her companion are on a mission and must not be delayed."

"How did ye know that?"

"Now is not the time for explanations, Wirt. Now is the time for leaving and continuing on our way."

"A mission. What kind of mission sends juves into Beyondness?"

"I am not at liberty to divulge such things."

"If you want to walk away with feet still attached to ankles, reveal all," Orsin said and the other three giants stepped forward, along with the slavering wolfies who bared their teeth and growled.

"They are to go beyond the Beyondness. To the place high up."

"We are?" I said and turned to Wirt who shook his head and moved in closer.

"I was to inform you when we arrived at a safe vicinity."

"Enough whispers between. Talk or lose some flesh."

"No talk so we can slice juicy meat form soft bits. Long time since we eat such delicacy," Marcellus said and grinned a nasty grin.

"No need for threats, their ultimate aim is to find the place where her bro and other Meeks have been taken."

Marcellus stepped back. "Our sis got took. We recall day well. She said she heard birdybird call name. Off she ran fast and fierce. We looked but she was gone."

"Keep such info inwards. These feebles need not know our business," Orsin said.

"Likewise," I blurted out. Orsin growled lower than the wolfies that prowled round his feet.

"Cross not, tiny fem, or we let loose wild ones."

"All this talk is keeping us from our purpose," Eadgard said and Orsin stepped in closer.

"Your tale has likeness to our own. I would hear more. You come to our place of living. Do not fear wolfies, they ours to command."

"A kindly offer, to be sure. But Adara, myself and Wirt must continue on."

"We not asking, we telling. Marcellus, take rear. We will escort humans. Walk!" Orsin commanded and I was all but ready to stay put, when I felt the hot breath of a wolfie on my ankle. Eadgard opened his mouth to speak, but was jabbed in the back with Orsin's whip. He turned to us and shrugged.

"We must do as we are told. I see no way out."

"I am more than willing to trudge on, just to be free of these Cloniewolves."

"Quiet. Keep walking," Marcellus said and off we tramped to who knows where.

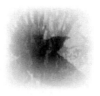

CHAPTER 13
The Clonie Zone

Wirt kept close to me and I to Eadgard. The fizzing light sticks the Clonies held cast a flickering light that made their shadows stretch out before them like long staccato cut-out puppets. I had seen such amusements when the Wanderers came to town. They set up a white cloth thing, shone a big round light behind it and set about making magic shapes with all manner of props and stuff. I was just a bub and thought it grand. This was not so much. This was all a-scary and for the first time since I began my journey, I wished I had not.

The further we walked the more unpleasant the surroundings became. What little I could see made me uneasy in the extreme. The flat ground became more uneven as we continued on. I became aware of lumps and bumps that were not formed from the dirt and ash that made up the soil in this place. The mounds I felt were hard and brittle and jutted up from the earth in gruesome shapes that could well have been the leftovers from a Carnie feast. I stepped upon something hard and it crunched beneath my feet. I glanced down and saw what looked like a broken arm, minus the skin and other living tissue. I shuddered, took a step back and cracked something else. This time I did not look down but carried on walking, trying not flinch each time I made contact with something dead. I noticed that when Wirt splintered a bone, he put both hands to his face and gave out little high-pitched squeaky noises that made Eadgard turn around and glare a disapproving glare at him. Wirt caught his eye, coughed all manly like and trod as close to me as a blind kittle to its mother.

The dazzling light that came from the Clonie torches illuminated more patches of the land we were travelling on. I glanced to my left and saw heaps of chewed up metal and hollowed out remains of what must have been rudimentary style houses. The gaps in the grey bricks where windows used to be made them look wide-eyed and afraid. I began to wonder if my face resembled them since I kept on letting my jaw drop each time I spied a charred skeleton strewn upon the earth. Perhaps the stories were true and the Clonies were cannibals.

I felt Wirt's lips close to my ear, "This could be a trap. They may be luring us to their lair so that they can dine upon our flesh."

"Happen so. I am beginning to a-worry about these folk."

"Clonies. For that is who they are," Wirt said, rather too loudly, for Marcellus came up behind and grabbed us by the shoulders.

"That name not name we call ourselves. That name given by likes of your tribe."

"Less noise from rear. We pass our sacred site. All bow heads and squeeze hands till they hurt, in respect of those that perished in last Agro war."

Marcellus let us go and I watched him lower his head and clench his hands together. He looked at us with a sideways head tilt and said, "Do same as we do, or Orsin will use whip to thrash you."

As soon as he said those words Orsin did indeed crackle his whip hard and we all bent our heads and wrung our hands until they almost bled. Beneath our feet were thousands of picked clean bones. Broken and hacked and bitten into. We tried to step over, but there were too many and they split and splintered when we stepped upon them. In the darkness and gloom the sharp snapping noise they made sounded like sulphur sticks on Bonfie Night. Although there was no wind as such, I felt a gust of mournfulness so cold and eager, that it whipped around my still fleshed bones and made me shiver. I began to think that these Clonies were maybe not so feral after all.

We crackled on, crunching bits of skeleton beneath, until the white fragments of long dead hominids thinned out and none were left.

Another ear piercing whip crack and Orsin spoke, "All heads high and proud. Tramp quick to destination. We taste Owl breath on our tongue."

Marcellus prodded us in the back and we stumbled forward quickening our pace. I nudged into Eadgard who grabbed my hand and said, "Owls are to be feared in these parts."

"Erhm, Adara," I said. "Catcher of birds. What do I have to fear? Or any of us, from any meat hungry Strigiform."

"They will have plucked out your eyes, heart and tongue before you had a chance to let rip your tune. This is the Beyondness. Things here are much mutated."

"This I would believe," I said and pulled Wirt with me.

I squinted into the distance and made out roundel shapes that I guessed were the domiciles of the Clonies. Orsin let rip with his whip again and the pack of snarling wolfies raced ahead. They stopped abrupt like when a ghostly figure emerged from the darkness. This creature was smaller than the other Clonies and wore a white robe that covered their entire body, all except for the face which resembled the flat roundness of an owlet. Minus the feathers and beak. The wolfies milled around the Clonie's legs and it bent to scratch-scratch the hound's ears and chin. Stranger than strange to see these fierce beasts become as docile dowgies in the hands of said Clonie. Orsin halted and turned to us.

"Enter our tribe and mind your voice. Speak if and when spoke to."

He was greeted with an embrace by the white-clad one. Orsin let his whip speak for him once more and the wolfies fled into the night. I felt a hand between my shoulder blades shove and my companions and I walked towards the Clonie camp. Wirt breathed hard and fast and I thought he might be weakening, so I gripped onto his hand. To my surprise he pulled it away and formed a fist.

"They will not eat me, or ye. Between us we can fight our way free. Of that I am sure," he said.

"Wirt, brave, yeah. Stupid also, yeah. Compose yourself before they smell your pique."

"Adara speaks sense. I do not believe the Clonies mean us harm," Eadgard said.

"Tales and stories and more I have heard about these things. They say that they snaffle their own as well as others."

"I have been scouting this territory for a full rotation and have never witnessed any such atrocity."

"All the same," Wirt said and clenched the other hand, "we best be on our guard."

"That goes without saying," Eadgard said and we ceased our tramping and stood before what could only be described as a female of the species.

The white-clad one spoke. "Welcome. I am Vea, in charge of all who abide within and without as far as eye can see. Enter and we shall eat."

"Not me ye won't, ye-" said Wirt all of a sudden and Eadgard had to wrap his arms around him to prevent a head on attack on Vea, who raised her arms into the air and lowered her lids.

"Let this simple boyman have peace," she said and pressed her palm against Wirt's forehead. He opened his gob all-wide as if to speak, but when nowt came forth. He closed said mush and to my shock horror, fell limp against Eadgard's chest.

Vea opened her eyes and stared at the slumped Wirt. He blinked and dragged his gaze from hers. His knees buckled and Eadgard lifted him into a standing position.

"Stand strong young'un," Eadgard said.

Wirt breathed in a huge lungful of air. His face became pale then red and he shook his head a few times before freeing himself from Eadgard's supportive grip. He walked slowly towards Vea, as if being pulled, and halted. She raised her chin a tad and stared down her tiny nose at Wirt. He knelt before her.

"Ye are a powerful force," he said and lowered his head. "Apologies."

"Taken in grace given. Now stand and all follow," she said and turned from us. Wirt stood and walked behind her like a faithful mutt.

I looked at Eadgard who returned my round-eyed stare with a look of bewilderment.

"What just happened here?"

Eadgard shrugged his shoulders. "Not sure. It is a puzzlement."

"How is it that she turned Wirt from antsy to calm in no more than a gnats breath?"

"Again, I cannot give an answer. He appears now to be unafraid. See how he follows the controlling fem as if they were recently reunited as friends?"

A thud on my back caused me turn and end our puzzled confab. I looked up and saw Orsin tower above me. I cringed at the weight of his touch and he lifted his great paw from my person.

"Come. Nothing to fear," he said. "Tramp close behind and all be well."

Eadgard and I exchanged a look of unsureness and followed Orsin towards the abode. The path we traipsed upon was lit either side by tall lamps that had flat oval glass tops. They gave out a shimmer rather than a glare and I guessed they were sun powered. We had similar solar illuminations in the Great Square at Cityplace and I began to wonder if the Clonies shared other things of tech. I saw a large dark structure in the distance surrounded by floor lights. They made a ring of light around its base that made it appear as if it were floating. So mesmerised by the uncanny sight was I, that I did not hear Marcellus creep up behind me.

"She mightiest of all. She strong. Cleverer than any that has or will live." He whispered.

I felt his hot, hot breath on my neck and shivered. He laughed and prodded me in the back. I stood still for a sec and took it upon myself to give him a goodly thwack the next time he chose to poke me thus. I turned to him with a thunderous face. He stared into my eyes and I swear behind the mask I saw a gentleness in his grey-blue orbs. I turned my head away from his intense stare and put my newfound soppiness down to the flattering light that bathed the area we stood in.

"Go quicker, Vea not tolerate tardy guest," he said and gave me a softly shove.

I was about to push him back with more violence than he showed me, when he took my hand all gentle-like and said, "Saying this so you will be saved from whipping."

"Ta for that," I said and I did not pull my hand away from his.

"Go. Friends already there."

"Right."

"Let go hand."

I looked down at our entwined fingers. Before my face glowed brighter than the lights that surrounded us, I snatched my hand from his and rushed to catch up with the others.

Wirt and Eadgard were standing at the portal of the Clonie home, a vast black tent in the shape of a dome. It must have been made from strong stuff as half the top had solar panels stuck to it. I marvelled again at the high-techness of such devices in this

soulless place. First the Ladies and now Clonies, all
with the same sort of gadgets that I thought only
existed in my hometown. Orsin pulled a flap open and
we walked inside.

"Wow!"

More Clonies, but not like the ones we
encountered on the outside. These were smaller,
slimmer and whiter. Their faces were as flat as Vea's,
with tiny noses and big round eyes. I wondered if
underneath their long-sleeved white robes that
reached the floor, they hid some hideous mutation. I
tugged my gaze from these extraordinary folk and
saw a whole load of stuff that I recognised.

Screens like the ones in Cityplace hung from the
top of the tent on thick wires. They were arranged in a
circle facing outwards so all could sit and stare from
any angle. They flickered on and off with images of
fabricated truths. Like the vids we sometimes
watched of persons and places other than our own.
Some of the locations I thought were familiar, and
indeed there in front of my eyes was the very centre
of Cityplace. But, it was not inhabited by any
Citydwellers I recognised.

Some of the Clonies were watching the screens,
sitting together on wooden benches with high backs.
They were holding hands or leaning affectionate-like
on each other's shoulders. Others were chit chatting
smiling and laughing.

I turned to face Wirt. His expression no doubt
matched my own in a look of wonderment, which
grew in intensity when we gawped at Orsin,
Marcellus and the other Clonies when they removed
their outer garments and masks. The hugeness we
came to fear outside was nothing more than a

costume. A goodly made one I grant, but still an illusion to scare us no doubt. Underneath their deceitful garb these scary males were not so dissimilar to the others. They wore a light grey all-in-one suit that clung to their lithe and sinuous frame. I watched in awe as they reached into their hip pockets, withdrew a grubby cloth and wiped off all their face paint. Underneath the makeup they were as white-faced and flat nosed as all the rest.

Marcellus noticed our amazement and came close, "Our disguise, sterling, yes?"

"Utterly," I said.

"But… But ye are Clonies?"

"All."

"Ye are not what I expected."

"Good."

Orsin leaned over Marcellus's shoulder and said, "If word of this is spread amongst outer camps, I will hunt you down and chew upon your flesh until there is no more than rancid grizzle. Our look indoors may not be as fierce, but our intent is, and always will be, to protect selves from those that would do us harm."

"And those would be?"

"You and your kind, Adara. Geneticists and scientists, Agros and anyone else's that believe in a place where monsters dwell. The Beyondness is ours."

"Ye can keep it," Wirt said and huddled close to Eadgard, who stepped discretely to one side.

"Where did you procure your screens?"

"That would give too much away, Girlie."

"I am not a girlie."

"I see you still are."

"Nah!"

"I hear raised voices," Vea said. "This not allowed indoors. In here all well. Any noise from anger and upset, must go out there where wind and time dispel its ferocity."

She put a hand upon my forehead and it felt as cool and soft as a bubs first kiss. I at once became all squidgy inside and do believe I smiled. She did too and her face became a glow of friendly. I squinted and thought I saw her expression change to that of frosty.

"Come, let us to place of serenity. Orsin tells me you share sorrow not unlike our own. It may come to pass that together we find solution to problem of Agros."

CHAPTER 14
A Common Enemy

Vea led us to an opening at the back of the tent. She pulled open a flap and I peered into a long corridor lit up by short stumpy peg lights that were stuck into the ground at regular intervals along the each side of the walls. They gave off a yellow glow as if the sun was trying to go down but was prevented from doing so. In between said lights were tall, thin, translucent poles that reached almost to the ceiling. They too gave off light in dim strips that fell onto the dirt floor in horizontal bands. I was almost tempted to play "oneleghop-hop" with them, but did not. I watched the others disappear down the passage but did not follow straight away. I lagged behind a bit growing uneasy with every slow step I took.

I stared into the amber orbs that protruded from the floor and became mesmerised by their swirling light. I squinted so as to be able to see what it was that swooshed around inside the round glass globs. It looked like some kind of thick ether or gas. My neck hairs twitched as if a chill swept over them and I jumped when a young Clonie bumped into my arm.

He smiled a wide-mouthed grin and I walked quicker, staying close to the long thin tubes that gave out a lowly hum. I brushed my hand down their surface and felt warmth. They were both heat and light. We had nowt so tech in all of Cityplace.

I picked up my pace and caught up with the others. My preoccupation at catching them caused me to stumble and I tripped upon something soft. "What the huff?" I said and all turned. There on the floor curled up between two heater poles, was a sleeping creature that resembled a kittlecat in every way except it had no ears.

"They too have pets?" Wirt said and bent to stroke the creature. It rolled onto its back and purred loudly at his touch.

"Ah you have found another of our secrets," Vea said and picked up the kittle. It snuggled its head into her chest and she kissed it as tenderly as if it were her own kiddle.

"What happened to its listening holes? Was it injured?"

"No, Adara, born that way. Same like your six fingers. Perhaps this place not so strange as you think?"

"Yep, it is and then some."

"Not to us. There are more than enough rejects here. We live as one, no harm comes to any." She pulled another heavy cloth covering open and we walked through it and into the night air.

This section of the Clonie camp was more organised. Huts and tents stood around a large square clearing that was partially hidden by a low fence made from scrap metal and bits of stone. Inside the rectangle were metal benches arranged to face the centre, almost like the seating in a place of entertainment. However, my curiosity at said structure diminished rapidly when a strange, unpleasant smell drifted up my nose passage. I turned to Wirt who was a-gagging at the stench. Even Eadgard showed some form of revulsion on his stony face, by screwing up his eyes and sticking his tongue out between his teeth. I held my hand over my mouth and tried not to breathe too deeply. Vea brushed past us and we followed her across a paved path to another black tent. This hut was smaller than the others, and seemingly the source of the gut-churning pong.

At the entrance, the kittle Vea was cradling jumped down and pushed itself through the heavy cloth flap that was the door. "She keen to feed and return to her family."

We followed the feline into the tent of food and a revolting smell came at us like a fart from a wolfie that has gulped down carrion. The dirt floor was strewn with bits of charred stuff that a group of kittles gnawed on. I gagged and Wirt closed his eyes. Eadgard swallowed hard.

"We keep kittlecats to protect food from vermin."

"What? You have rodents?" Eadgard said.

"Certainly. Always around edibles."

"I have never seen any animal other than wolfies and raptors here," Eadgard said.

"They do not venture into wild. They present little problem. Their numbers are few. Besides, in world bereft of most of Mother Nature's inhabitants, even rats and mice are welcome sight."

"This place is almost a dream. I am thinking that I am not here but in the land of slumber where all my fears and hopes are jumbled. So confused am I," Wirt said and held his head in his hands.

"Come. Let us sit in quiet and partake of sustenance. You must be weary and hungry after journey."

"I am most readily, great Missus," I said all energetic like. Then shut my mouth quickly. I did not know why I blabbed such info and began to wonder if Vea had some strange way of making me say what she wanted to hear. Wirt gave me a look of "What the huff did you say that for?" and I shrugged.

"Do nay bother yerself with our needs," Wirt said.

"You have own sustenance?"

"Erhm, well, we did, but I left our goodie pouch behind when first we met with yer kind."

"The loss is no matter. We not see you go without."

Vea smiled and gestured for us to sit on black metal chairs around a huge round grey stone table. We did and hung onto the edge as if we were giddy. I looked across the room and saw a huge black stove with many burners and three ovens. I suspected these Clonies liked to cook. In Cityplace, the nearest we got to preparing our own food was to rip open a packet and heat it in the micro.

"There is a choice of edibles. Sheeple stew or roast chikkie."

On Vea's last word, "chikkie," Wirt chucked up.

"Meat!" he said through gasps and kicked soil over the offending bile.

"Of course. You have seen terrain. Not much veg can grow out here."

"But there have been no sheeples on any land for centuries. Chikkles here and there, but only as pet. Their flesh is poison tainted by the still-active virus."

"Rejects remember. Experiments gone wrong. Flung out to fend for ourselves as best we can. What you see around are things unwanted. Because of looks, or flavour, or yield. These creatures we consume were bred for that purpose. They bear little resemblance to namesakes. Flavour is sour to be sure, but we have means and ways to gain spices and herbs so that taste not too unpleasant."

Wirt coughed and twitched his over sensitive nose. His face turned a fine shade of green. He pulled at his shirt sleeve and held it over his gob as a shield against the ever-growing pong that hovered in the air.

"How do you come by all this animal?" I asked between coughs.

"We are given it to keep quiet. After the foray that killed many, the remnants you will have walked amongst. We became good at war, better than Agros. So we agree compromise. Agros leave us and in return we test new forms of meat, before they dare consume for themselves."

"Meat, meat, meat. Can ye desist from uttering the word? I am aghast and agape with it all and cannot believe what I have heard and smelt."

"Ah, Wirt. You are tender in all things we think. Come, eat. We venture you will not be so upset when you taste food."

He wafted her away with his free arm and stood. "Never. I am Woodsfolk and will never digest animals that are made as nothing more than living meat. It is beyond the cruellest of cruelties to modify so."

"You stare at such a modification, boy," Vea said.

"That may be, but I would not eat ye."

"We should hope not."

"I would not eat any meat."

"You're convictions are solid. We respect this."

Wirt flopped back down and buried his head in his arms. Vea folded hers and I caught a glint of anger appear in her eyes, so in an attempt to extinguish said fire, I said, "You know what? I have journey food with me that I will be glad to munch upon so that you do not need to plunder your resources." Wirt gave me thumbs up sign and sank his head back down.

"Do not offend our hospitality," Vea said and her face lost its look of friendly. She turned to Wirt and bent low over his shoulder. "We have greenery if you prefer?"

He lifted his noggin and turned his pallid face to hers. It was a fierce countenance that she presented him with. I doubt that Wirt could refuse her offer. He gulped and said, "What sort? Fresh or engineered?"

"Bit of both. We grow some veg. A hardy variety that can thrive in this unyielding soil. Mostly we use to feed critters we consume. But it has flavour and packed full of necessary nutrients. It resembles most what you would call carrot."

Wirt sat upright and tried to grin. The widening of his lips however, came out more of a grimace than a grin. Vea frowned and Wirt quickly said, "Ye make it sound quite edible. I most definitely will try some."

"Adara, Eadgard, will you partake?"

I looked at Eadgard and said, "My Santy Breanna would no doubt give me wallop, but despite the unrest in my belly and nose, I will be as daredevil and try a mouthful."

"Eadgard?"

"I have never eaten meat. I confess to being somewhat curious as to its flavour. I too will consume some of this genetically produced product."

"Then we will bring you a portion of each. And for Wirt, soup made from our homegrown root plant," Vea said and headed towards a large metal cooker.

Wirt stared at us both and shook his head. "I am appalled at ye both. How can ye eat of creatures made from who knows what? Living things that no doubt screamed in pain when they were butchered. I shudder at the hideous thought."

"Now, Wirt, these things are bred for nothing else. I would assume they cannot feel anything, including pain or fear at the thought of death," Eadgard said.

"Ye do not know this, ye cannot."

"I understand yer upset, Wirt," I said and went to hold his hand, but he pulled away and lowered his head. Vea approached and placed several dishes and spoons onto the table. The stuff upon them looked like Wirt's puke and if I am honest, smelt like it too. I took a deep breath, picked up a spoon and had my first taste of meat. My throat contracted spontaneously as the mushy stuff slid down. The only thing I could compare the taste to was cheese gone bad, then left to decompose.

Vea watched our every move, arms folded and her face as stern as before. When we had swirled the concoction around our bowls and lifted and sniffed and tasted but a lickfull, she straightened her back and said, "Well? What do you think?"

Eadgard stared at his food, Wirt closed his eyes and I being the only one left that had no idea of how to answer, found myself unable to make up a fitting pretence at how I felt.

Under the table, Eadgard's foot made contact with my shin and I blurted forth, "If I am honest, I think it tastes of something passed from out my innards." I placed my spoon upon the table and pushed the bowl away, expecting a cuff or something worse from Vea's hand. She made no movement or angry sound. Instead she turned to Eadgard, who to my wonderment, was spooning more of the nasty stuff into his gob.

"Eadgard, you have taken more than one mouthful. Is it to your liking?"

"It is not unpleasant. Neither is it pleasant. I think that if I had no other source of grub, then I would partake of this again."

Vea turned her raptor stare upon Wirt. He moved his spoon around the contents of his bowl, shook his head, gulped in air and delved into the slimy slop that Vea placed before him. We watched as his face contorted into spasms of grimaces until, at last, he swallowed.

"By the Greenman himself I have never tasted anything so vile," he said.

"Our opinion is you are used to different fare. What you dislike is all we know."

Wirt, to his unbounded credit, took another breath and swallowed up all the mess that was in his bowl. He gagged but once and sat back, his face all red from the hurry. Vea slapped his back and all as one we laughed.

"A fine fellow you are, Wirt," said Eadgard.

"Indeed he is," I said and found myself resorting to the mumsy-feel I had when first we met.

Vea turned to Eadgard. "If you all done, we would speak of your quest."

"A thing we are keen to resume. It is my duty to escort these young 'uns and I would not fail them by being late."

"Late for what?"

"Excuse, Adara, I blabber on too frequent."

"Blabber more," I said and stood.

"Adara, sit and let me tell story that may be familiar," Vea said and despite my wrath at Eadgard's holding forth of information, I dutifully sat. There was a commanding nature to Vea, a solidness of purpose that manifested itself in how she talked and moved. So that I could not help but obey when she spoke. And although not at all at ease in her presence, I found myself unable to resist any request she made.

"In our most recent past, spate of abductions take place. You must understand, we outcasts, feared, loathed. We perpetuated our monster image to preserve our way of life. And for some time this has been case. Our horror at missing bubbas has shaken very foundations of our society. Instead of calm and merry, anger and unhappiness spread like fungus. When you related purpose in our land, we knew you would assist in gaining our loved ones back."

"Why cannot you discover your own by yourselves?"

"Eadgard, we cannot travel beyond Beyondness. Criterion for survival was permanent promise to stay put. We should not exist. Government way back made scientists swear to destroy us all."

"Wait for one sec," I said. "All know there are Clonies in the Beyondness."

"Hideous mutants that feed on hominid flesh?" Vea asked.

"I get yer meaning."

Vea sat next to Wirt and closed her eyes for a sec. When she opened them we saw a tear or two run down her cheeks. The change from stern to sad was unsettling, so were the words she spoke next.

"I would have you add to your gang one of us, so we can rescue four of our own taken ones."

"Impossible. I have orders that I cannot, will not disobey," Eadgard said.

"Not even to save young lives?"

"Your hurt is most sad and unfortunate, but my mission… My orders are very specific."

"We assumed you would be freeing all who were taken."

"With only us three to do the rescuing? That would be a plan to fail."

"With extra fierce one at side you might have better chance?" Vea said and all eyes turned to Eadgard.

"This is most irregular. I have my orders."

"Change them."

"I could I suppose."

"You must have phonespeak access to your commander?"

"I do, but can only use it once and then only in an emergency."

"The lives of many young ones is emergency, we think."

Eadgard turned to face me. He gave me a look as if to ask for my support and although I was a-keen to leave and find my bro-bro, I found myself on her side. I stood and folded my arms to show that I meant business and said, "Vea, add one on to us and we will save your bubs and bring them back. Do not object, Eadgard. This we must do."

"Adara, what ye say? Why ye say?"

I had no response that made a tad of sense to answer Wirt. I merely stood my ground and said, "It is the right thing to do. I know it."

Eadgard put his head in his hands for a moment, and then looked up. "Vea, the screens you use to watch your homegrown vids, do they have a channel to communicate?"

"There is one that has a signal that leads to without. You may use it to speak to those you need to."

"Then let us to it. For time is running short."

"Good decision made. We will to home tent and settle matter."

"Vea?" I asked. "Whom do you consider suited to the journey ahead?"

"Ah, you have already met, Adara."

"Marcellus?"

"Well guessed."

"Oh plop," I said.

CHAPTER 15
Rank and File

We went back to the home tent and Vea took Eadgard to a comscreen that was hidden behind a brown cloth hanging. Wirt and I stood without speaking. He watched the Clonies watching the vidscreen, whilst I searched the room for a sight of Marcellus. I was strangely sad that I did not see him there.

I felt an itch on my ankle, bent to scratch it and saw a kittle claw at its neck. It made sense that lice would be abundant in such a place. I was about to let Wirt in on the presence of fleas when Vea emerged from behind the screen. She took my arm.

"You must not travel in such flimsy attire. Come with me to wash place. We conjure up clothes better suited."

"Kindly gesture, but I have heavier garb with me. I would be glad of a space not overlooked to change into it, though."

"Come with me," she said and I left Wirt and followed her out of the home tent past the food place to a tall brown shack fashioned from all manner of oddments. The walls and roof were made from corrugated metal and the door looked like it came from one of the ghost houses we saw as we passed through the bone site. Vea pulled it open and I saw rows of open cubicles with holes in the ground. The only light came from two large windows in the middle of the roof. I could not help wondering if they could be opened for there was a general smell of plop in the air. I pinched my nose and cautiously stepped in.

"See at back?" Vea said and pointed to a large screen that blocked the entire back wall. "That is where we dress after cleansing. You see to right, long channel in floor?" I nodded. "Drainage. Look up." I did. "See in ceiling pipe with holes in? Water pours down, we all wash."

"When you say, 'we all wash', you mean more than one at a time?"

"Certainly. Save water that way. We do not fear sight of flesh from own."

Vea's words were sensible enough and I took my leave of her. I walked past the poo chambers to the screen at the back and slid behind it. There was a long low stone bench attached to the wall and above that, a row of metal hooks. No doubt to hang one's clothes upon. I turned my head and looked from left to right, just to make sure no Clonie were present and took off my tattered frock.

"I leave you to dress in private," Vea said.

I hastily delved into my Synthbag and pulled out a heavy pair of pants and shirt. I peeled off my once-pretty dress and left it on the stone bench behind me. I shook my weightier garments, turning my head away from the cloud of dust that wafted from them and when satisfied they were as clean as they could be, I sat on the bench and placed my right leg into the troos. I heard a dull sound as if someone was plonking themselves onto a chair and paused. I listened again. Nowt. The strangeness of the place was playing tricks on my ears. I smirked, pulled on the pants and shirt and stepped out from behind the screen. Vea was gone. Yet I swore I could hear breathing. I held my breath and listened. I looked around the place but it was empty. I was overcome with a sense of being watched and shivered. Not wanting to remain any longer in this echoey space, I secured my Synthbag on my back and hurried past the no-door poo places. I yanked open the door, stepped out into the cleaner air and saw Wirt and Eadgard standing by the food hut, all huddled together and deep in chat.

"I am not keen to have this Clonie with us," Eadgard said.

"I adhere to yer opinion."

"They are abounding in subterfuge and therefore not to be trusted."

"Ye are right."

"I can hear all that you are a-saying, despite your whisperings," I said, walked over to Wirt and Eadgard and stood between them. They were gasbagging just outside the exit flap of the eating-place. Both had wrinkled brows and down turned mouths, which made them look as though they had once more eaten of the gloop Wirt had so bravely consumed. They turned when they heard me speak and I attempted a friendly smile. It was met with frowns.

"Adara, you do not appear to be so much worried by the addition of this Marcellus."

"I am not enamoured by the prospect of his company. He presented a fierce and unfriendly face to us in the Beyondness to be sure. But to his credit, he gave me some well-needed and heeded advice. I am inclined to think that for all their growls and spit-spat ways, these Clonies are an honourable bunch."

Wirt gave me a wide-eyed look and stood closer to Eadgard, who picked dirt out from underneath his fingernails with his teeth. I took such a gesture to mean that he was ambivalent about the situation, despite his earlier words. When Wirt spoke, there was no such doubt.

"Humph and piffle. Ye have been amongst these folk for nothing more than a few heartbeats. I grant that Vea has a power that sets the senses reeling so that ye cannot tell what from what, and more, no longer care. But that I think it is a power that can just as easily be used to harm as well as heal."

"Wise words, Wirt," Eadgard said.

"Indeed. I have chill neck too and then some, but also a niggle-naggle in my nonce that tells me they are more than their sum," I said. "Besides, he is to come and that is that. No use grieving and sulking and the like. If we encounter something bizarre and threatening, what better creature to have as companion than one who knows this place and calls it home?"

"Ye have all the answers," Wirt said, then hung his head and set about moving dirt with his foot. I looked to Eadgard; he wiped his face with his hand and took a long look at my person.

"Good to see that you have changed into more suitable attire," he said.

I smoothed down my heavy Synthowool tunic and brushed muck from the bottom of my thickly woven troos. When I stood straight again, I saw Marcellus approach from the cleansing hut. The feeling of being spied upon returned. But it soon disappeared when he waved to us all in such a friendly manner. And despite our earlier misgivings, we all smiled back. He stood tall before us and grinned.

"All ready for leavings?"

"To be sure," I said and noticed how different his face looked when his mouth was upturned. It took on an almost innocent appeal and I felt all-jolly for a moment. That is until Wirt gave him such a glare that I was compelled to reprimand him for his lack of geniality.

"Do not fret, Wirt. We go in front, you leave gap as big as you think fit."

"That is where I draw the line," Eadgard said and stepped forward. "I am the Backpacker here and I am the only person that knows the place where we are to go. I will lead. Let there be no mistake."

"We step aside then," Marcellus said.

"That is how it shall be from now on. I will always walk in front, Adara behind me, Wirt behind her and you, Marcellus; keep to the rear."

I nodded and Wirt put his hands on his hips. Marcellus wiped his tiny nose on the back of his hand and lifted a large brown sac over his shoulder. It looked full and heavy and I wondered if he was hoarding some of that genomeat we had tasted earlier. Part of me was curious as to what the creatures that it came from looked like. Apparently my thoughts became words without me knowing, for out of the tent came Vea carrying what can only be described as a pink legless blob. Wirt stepped back and I gulped down what I had eaten before.

"In answer to earlier query, here is what we call chickie," Vea said and held it out. "Do not be afraid. It will not bite. No teeth, no need. Gums are hard though."

The creature wriggled in her arms and she set it upon the ground. It wobbled then stretched out so that a sort of head and stumpy neck appeared. Two green eyes blinked and I saw a pair of holes below them contract then blow out dust. It opened its mouth (a lipless slit underneath the nostrils) and made a clicking noise that sounded like it was reprimanding us all for something we had yet to do wrong.

"What a sad and sorry thing," Eadgard said.

"It is well taken care of as are all animals in our care."

"An abomination against Mother Nature herself is what it tis," Wirt said and turned away.

"Kind Wirt, you are too sensitive. Do not fret about this creature or others. They not wise to their plight. We not butcher animals. They modified to live certain time and then they simply stop."

"All the same," I said, "to what we are used to, they do appear unnatural and grotesque."

Vea walked up to me and took my hand. She placed it onto her face and said, "As did we to you. Have you changed mind about us?"

"Yes."

Wirt pulled my hand away from Vea's cheek. He stood facing her and said, "Not the same. Most of yer strangeness came from costumes and forced aggression."

"Point is made however. Do not condemn others to your interpretation of what you imagine them to be." Vea held out her hand for Wirt to take, but he brushed it aside.

"Words, words, words. Ye are all too keen to talk ye way out of dark doings. Do not come near me, good woman, I fear ye will taint my mind to acquiescence like ye did before. I will retain my own thoughts however much they disagree with yours."

Marcellus loomed over Wirt and held up a mighty fist, "Not speak to our great Lady in this fashion, or we will-"

Vea stood in between the two, grasped Marcellus's arm and gently lowered it.

"Marcellus, hush. This boy soft and gentle and must not be abused. All journey together. Behave and help, not judge. Have we taught you nothing?"

Marcellus took a deep breath and Vea smiled.

I turned my attention away from them and onto Eadgard. Who, all the while they were jabbering, had been squatting on the floor and stroking the chickie as if it were his pet. I hoped that I concealed my look of disgust at his actions and dared to speak of our most impending mission.

"If all are finished and done a-bickering, may we take to our heels and continue to travel?"

Eadgard rose and straightened his back. "Well said, Adara. This place has a strange effect upon me. Let us move before our tardiness causes us to miss our rendezvous."

"We not be cause of bother on travels. This we pledge," Marcellus said and bowed to Vea.

"This happy news to our ears. We trust Marcellus not meet with further hostility from your companions?"

"This I pledge on behalf of Adara, Wirt and myself, Vea. We will be as kin and watch each other's behind."

"If I find anyone a-looking at my nethers, I won't be afraid to give out clout," Wirt said and all but he chortled at his remark. "I do not jest. This ye know."

He looked in my direction and I lowered my head in shame. Not so much time had passed since Wirt was set upon and defiled. I ceased my jollification.

"Eadgard, let us on our way."

"With all pleasure. Many thanks for the use of your communication system."

"Glad to be assistance. Much fortune on your quest. Return to us swelled with those we have lost. Take provisions offered and do not be squeamish as to their origin," Vea said and gave us all a package.

"Thanks to you and bye-byes for now," I said and found myself impelled to hug her.

She clasped me close and I heard unspoken words fill my head. Warnings about the dangers of our trip. I could not cipher them exact, so all I got was a sense of doom and foreboding. Which really was of no help at all. Vea released me and Eadgard nodded in respect, then headed toward the black Beyondness. We followed in the order previously assigned.

CHAPTER 16
We Take Flight

Although the sky is the same all over, I swear out here it was darker. Darker and a nasty shade of navy blue. Sounds the like I have not encountered caused me to twitch and jump. The moon, what there was of it, shone so dimly that I found it more than tricky to keep sight of Eadgard. I could hear Wirt mumbling and grumbling at just about everything and caught a name spat out here and there, sure in the knowledge that Marcellus could also make out his moniker between profanities. I turned from time to time in the hope of engaging Wirt's eye and giving him a look of friendliness, but the black we moved in all but obliterated his shape.

A shriek as shrill and loud as a bub in a hissy scratched into our ears and Eadgard told us to fall down until he gave the signal all clear. I tasted dust and curled into a ball hoping Wirt would do the same. The raptor shrieks came close. I swear I felt the rush of wind across my back from wings flapping nearer than I would have liked. I turned my head to the side and saw the earth around me swirl as talons plucked the ground. I made myself smaller, buried my head in my hands and waited for the hideous creatures to leave. Their screeches swept across my squidged up form and I was almost close to giving way to a fearful scream when their sound dissolved into the diminishing night.

I slowly lifted my head and saw Eadgard rise from the ground.

"All gone. Get up," he said and reluctantly we did. "Come, we must continue forth."

I swiped away the dust from my clothes and when I straightened myself, felt Wirt engirdle my waist with his arm. I was glad to have it there and even gladder that he had ceased to be all crisscross with me. Eadgard waved us on and Wirt and I followed. I turned and saw Marcellus walk a few paces behind. I smiled for no reason and he returned my gesture with a grin that made his face appear strong and friendly all at the same time. Wirt noticed my gaze. He made a snort and pulled me to face the front. And on we tramped through the ash to where only Eadgard knew.

Clouds heavied the sky and our only source of illumination went out. "Stop. Do not move until I furnish us with luminance until the sun rises, which cannot be much longer now," Eadgard said and I heard a crack and hissing noise come from his direction. In an instant all was bright. Eadgard held the dandiest torch lamp in front and it illuminated our way as though the sun was shining through it. Even though the only thing it shined upon was dirt and dust and…

"We are here," Eadgard said and shone the lamp upon a humungous grey flat wall.

"I have a feeling vile about this place." Wirt whispered into my left ear.

"Don't be such a bubs. I'm sure all will be as fine as a kittle close to sleep."

"When we enter you must not look directly at the light in front of you. It is not for viewing. It is a slight malfunction of the overall ambient lighting that was issued to these crafts as a prototype. This particular model broke. Unfortunately there was not time to mend it. It dazzles, be warned."

"So, I am a bubs am I?"

"Step back whilst I enter the code," Eadgard said and produced a small black thingamabob from his leg band. We inched closer gathering so near his shoulder that he almost lost his balance.

"Did I not inform you to step back?" We did. "And do not watch as I tap." We did not.

A whoosh like that from a raptor swooping filled our ears and blew across our faces as the wall slid apart to reveal a grey corridor, at the end of which was a blinding white light that seemed to hover above the floor.

"Do not look into it. Bend your heads and follow my feet."

Eadgard led the way, head lowered so as not to peer into the brightness. Wirt, Marcellus and myself entered also. Wirt made sure that I was next to the Clonie and stayed close to my side as we walked. He shielded his face with his hand and Marcellus produced a pair of shades and put them on. I chose to look upon the floor and thus we stepped gingerly along the metal corridor.

It was a wide passage, smooth and devoid of any ornament. I could not get a goodly look since my eyes saw mostly ground and other people's feet, but the air was stale and somewhat warm. The white radiance became brighter the nearer we got to it. I could feel its heat upon my exposed neck and put my hand against my nape to prevent further scorching of my flesh. I longed to lift my head but heeded well the caution Eadgard spoke of and kept my gander down.

"Halt and keep your eyes averted from the source. I am about to attempt to shut it down," Eadgard said and we stopped. I heard a tip-tapping like when Eadgard punched in some numbers on his thingy outside and the light went out. "Now you can look."

I raised my head and saw that I was standing next to the light that had so dazzled us. It was big and round and jutted out from the wall and if I were in a playful mood, I would have hid behind it and let the others try to find me. I turned my gaze to straight ahead and let my mouth drop open for a sec. In front of me, and behind a square opening, was the cockpit of an aircraft. I dimly remembered seeing a vid of said space in ancienthistory class. I was not so overawed by the switches and knobs back then. But seeing such tech in the flesh, as it were, caused my heart to flip-flop.

The control panel that stretched right across beneath the front window was filled with dials and buttons and screens displaying who knows what. In the middle of the dashboard was a big metal handle jutting out in a horizontal fashion. Two big, black, padded chairs faced said controls and each had small levers attached to the side. Behind those seats were three more. They were not so comfy looking, being less padded and a garish shade of green. Wirt grabbed my arm and I his and together, as if we were as one, we said, "Metal birdybird!"

"Must you speak in infant babble?" Eadgard said.

We peered into the room and Marcellus pushed his head between ours. "This something rare. We never see jetliner before. Heard one once we think. Few moon cycles ago. About time we first see Eadgard. Vea said big boom noise was plane, like we see in one of vidramas. We thought her full of quip and did not take her words seriously. Now we see all this, realise how wise a female she is. We are in awe, we are in joy. We are in fear also, we think."

"Yes, yes, I'm sure it is all-new and wondrous, but there is no time for all this chatter. Please quieten your thoughts and mouths and each take a seat."

Marcellus entered the room first and went directly to one of the comfy chairs. We followed and Eadgard stood at the entrance for a sec. Marcellus was about to sit down when Eadgard stormed in and said, "Not the seat on the left, Marcellus, that is the captain's chair. Which is mine."

Marcellus shuffled over to the adjacent seat.

"Not the one next to it either. That is the co-pilot's chair. You may sit in any of the green ones behind," Eadgard said.

Marcellus grunted and plonked himself down in the middle of the three rear chairs. Eadgard sat in his captain's place and strapped himself into the high backed black chair. He faced the row of dials and knobs and levers and things I didn't even know existed, and began to fiddle with them in a most expertly way. I sat to the right of Marcellus and Wirt sat to his left behind Eadgard. Although the seats did not look to be as padded as the ones in front, once my butt touched down upon them they felt as comfy as a mumsy's lap.

"Do as I have just done and put your safety belt on. As you can see from the window, night is fading fast and daybreak is but a whisper away. Once the sky is lit we will be on our way. Do not be alarmed too much by what will happen next. Expect much noise and vibration. And please, Wirt, attempt to keep your mouth shut and not to shriek in terror when we leave the ground."

"Do not concern yerself with my behaviour. I am used to being high up. I've been climbing trees since I could use my legs and feet."

"Glad to know you have a head for heights. For those who may not, there is a sturdy container stuck underneath your seat. Please use it to throw up in and not barf all over the place."

At that point I began to pop with tiny beads of perspiration. Wirt noticed my pale demeanour and held onto my hand. Marcellus gripped onto the arms of his chair. I saw the side of his neck show signs of anxious too, as drops of wet slid down, and I smelt the pungent stench of sweaty fear escape from his direction. I looked to the glass in front and saw the dark sky lighten. Through a crack in the grey clouds, the sun appeared and the outside world began to brighten. I made myself ready for flight by stiffening every muscle in my already tense body.

"All ready?"

"Ay Captain, all ready," said Wirt all loud and fearless.

"Good. Hold on if you need to. We are taking off in… Three, two, now!"

Eadgard pressed and pushed and prodded all manner of protuberances and the flying machine began to hum and judder. I felt my insides flip and flounder and leant well back into my seat. The growling roar of what must have been the engine firing up, filled my entire body with their infernal racket. If my fingers had not been so busy clinging onto Wirt's forearm, I would have plunged them into my aching ears. I tensed and held my breath as the thing began to move. I heard another noise above the din, a thin and whining sound like a bub that had fallen and scraped its knee. I managed to turn my head and look at Wirt to see if he were making it, but his mouth was all upturned and he was leaning forward with a look of utter joy upon his face. I cocked my ear towards Marcellus and found the source of whimper. Like me he was afraid and found it impossible to hide the fact.

I forced myself to look out of the window to my side and could not help but mewl like Marcellus when the solid ground below was replaced by nowt but air. Dear Wirt was quicker than a hunter spider after a fly, and had the puke sac under my chin before I even knew I was to barf. I let all that I had eaten for the past few days escape my quivering tum and slumped against the headrest.

Marcellus's right hand dug into the back of Eadgards chair, whilst his left did the same to the co-pilot's. His bulk was hunched between the two front seats and my ears caught the sound of what can only be described as a loud and viscous chunder.

"I am going to have to ask you to clean that up, Marcellus. I can't quite see the instruments for the film of vomit you have managed to cover them with," Eadgard said.

Then I saw Marcellus's back convulse and heard him give the control panel one more goodly coat.

CHAPTER 17
The Monastery in the Clouds

The pungent of pong of vom caused me to hurl once more and I hung over the edge of the seat, my head buried deep into the spew pouch. Amidst dry retches I heard the sound of a fan and was more than relieved when it turned out to be an extractor device that sucked away all the bad air. I sat up and Eadgard turned to me.

"I believe you have a Synthbag? This is good. No doubt there is something inside that can calm and soothe both you and Marcellus?"

I managed to grunt an affirmation to Eadgard's query and let Wirt fumble around my shoulders until he came across the invisible satchel. As soon as he pulled it free the clever piece of tech became as visible as all around it. Through half closed eyes I saw Eadgard rub his chin and nod his head.

"I have heard of these wonders but not until this moment have I seen one. You will allow me to search for suitable medication?"

"No. Let Wirt. He has already come across some things of privacy I would not wish to have revealed to others gathered here," I said and limply waved my hand towards Wirt.

He grinned as if he were to open a prezzie and carefully rummaged through the contents. He pulled out a sac with a red cross on it and handed it to Eadgard.

"With your permission I will administer meds to both you and Marcellus."

"Please do and make it quick. I think I am to spew again," I said and took a deeply breath.

"Are these correct?" Eadgard said and hovered a small sachet in front of my bleary eyes.

"They are. Half the contents each in water."

"Wirt, would you be so kind as to assist me?"

"A pleasure. Although I would rather not administer cure to the Clonie."

"Understood. I will tend to his needs."

Sweet Wirt, all a-gentle, held my head whilst I supped the brew. In not more than a heartbeat I was free of sick and bother. I wiped my face with my hand and witnessed Marcellus take the drink from Eadgard, who despite his misgivings about said Clonie, attended to him as if he were one of us. Marcellus coughed twice then turned to me all smiles.

"We who have some tech to speak of, have nothing so instant, fine as this. Where you procure such meds?"

"Dunno. We have them that's all. Each month a new supply to fill them arrives and we are given our allocations. As to their origin, I can only guess. The Agros give us all our needs. Except for now. Now they withhold and deprive us of stuff we once took for granted."

"They troublesome, cruel. We forced to deal with them to survive, but they do bad things in past and present. We continue to war in heads with these all-governing folk."

"They have the power all right. Ye can be sure. I have no liking for them."

"You are not alone in your feelings. Many others have become less feared and more disillusioned. The day will come when-"

"Wait. Eadgard, if you are standing giving aid, who is steering the craft?" I said in a voice all-high in alarm.

"Calm yourself, Adara. Once fired into action and course plotted in, this machine flies itself. I will be needed merely to land."

"When will that be?" Marcellus said.

"Very soon."

"Good. We would prefer to be on ground."

"Shame for me as I have thrilled upon this part of the journey," Wirt said and peered out of the cockpit window. "All I can see are clouds. White, and big, and fluffy. Nay wait." He leaned closer to the glass. "The clouds have thinned. I think I can make out some giant rock things. I have never seen such hugeness of hill before. I wish ye would take a look, Adara. The tops are all pointy and covered with white." He pulled his face away from the scenery and said, "Where are we exactly?"

Eadgard stiffened for a moment. "I am not at liberty to confide this information. All that I can tell you is that we are at the highest point in all of NotSoGreatBritAlbion."

"High? You have more meds to share, Adara? We not used to such lack of ground level and fear we succumb to retchedness again."

"More than enough for us all," I said in reassurance to Marcellus.

"If ye are both fixed, then come and look. The earth looks wondrous great from so far up. I feel almost like a birdybird myself."

Marcellus and I stood shakily and went to gaze through the window with Wirt. It was indeed a splendid sight. Through the hazy clouds, snow-tipped mountains appeared vast and solid and as cold and desolate as any place I had ever seen. Both in 3D and 2D vids.

"We have never witnessed hugeness of rock before," Marcellus said and pressed his hand against the strengthened glass. I noticed that his fingers were long and slender. His hands too were slim and gentle looking, such a contrast to the guise they wore to scare outsiders. The more I saw of these Clonies, the more they became a mystery. I wished to ask and question him about all sorts of things, but the time was not fitting. So instead I too marvelled at the craggy hills that rolled out before us.

"We will land shortly," Eadgard said and sat back down in his Captain's chair.

"We will? But where? I have read that these vast planes need long flat stretches to put down on. Unless I witnessed something different from the rest, all these mounds of rock are spiky, tall and craggy." My voice became all-high again and I dug my fingernails into the arm of the chair. "Therefore, unsuitable as a place to land."

"Do not concern yourself, Adara. This marvellous piece of engineering can set down on any surface. So if you will all buckle up once more," he said and we did, "I will safely land us."

"Upon one of these barren mountains?"

"Yes, Marcellus. But not all are quite so sterile as the summits you have eyed today. One last look ahead and you will see something quite remarkable."

We all squinted through the murky pane. Into view came an enormous turreted construction perched on top of a particularly high mountain. It was white as the clouds that swirled around it and I gasped at the sight.

"Prepare for landing. It may be somewhat bumpy," Eadgard said.

We sat back down and buckled ourselves in. I leant back into the chair and stiffened throughout as the aircraft changed position from horizontal to vertical. I felt my ears sing and pop as we plummeted towards the ground.

Thanks to the meds I had taken earlier, I kept the contents of my stomach inside, not out. I closed my eyes and clenched onto the corners of my seat and felt gravity sweep up towards my cheeks and push them this way and that. I took in short breaths and thought I would yell some, but a bouncing of wheels on earth made me keep tight my lips. The engine noise powered down into a continuous drone then stopped. I opened my eyes to see Wirt unbuckling my seat belt and grinning like a lovesick Newly.

"Ye should have kept yer eyes unclosed. What wondrous things to witness. Clouds flying past as quick as lightening. And the ground zooming nearer and nearer and-"

"Do not proceed further with description. We used up all power of will not to let innards out upon this rapid descent," Marcellus said.

"Bubs, all of ye. Ye will not take the thrill of this adventure away from me with your mewling ways," Wirt said.

"Come. We are here," Eadgard said, and undid his belt.

"Exactly where is here?"

"On top of the world, Adara," he said and got up from his seat.

"Well that says nothing," I said and stood. Too abruptly, as it turned out. All blood seemed to drain from my head and in a dizzy faint I stumbled forward into the arms of Marcellus. He was quick to grab and stop me falling, but unfortunately for him, the bits of me he held in his hands were my mamms. I came-to in a shot and just before I swiped his gob, I saw a look of terror on his face.

"Sorry, pardon. We apologise. Not in many lifetimes would we have rested upon your plump bits. Accident, accident."

"When you two have finished doing your merry little dance, we have people to meet and things to see," Eadgard said and strode with purpose towards the corridor. He stopped at the exit. "One thing you will need to know, this establishment is holy. Those that live here are holy too. Give them respect."

"Ye mean this is a monastery?"

"Of sorts."

"There are monks here that believe in the Onegreatbeing?"

"Amongst others."

"What others?"

"Wirt, desist with all the queries. You sound like a crawler begging info from its mam."

"At least I care as to our whereabouts. Those two seem unaware, so engrossed in each other's bits."

"We not engrossed. She fell, we caught, is all. Keep unclean thoughts to yourself, half male."

"I am all male. Do not call me half, ye who cried like a-"

"Enough bickering. Let us go. Now follow me as close as is convenient. Do not speak unless spoken to. And above all else, to those who cannot endure heights, do not look over the mountain tops."

Eadgard entered the corridor and we followed, this time in single file. The passage that had seemed so bright and wide and long looked smaller in the light of dawn. The metal floor and walls and ceiling that had appeared all alien and forbidding, became nothing more than a simple gangway which led to the exit. Eadgard paused at the doorway and turned to us with a solemn look upon his face.

"It will be windy and cold so brace yourselves," Eadgard said and one by one, we stepped out of the aircraft and into the raw, fresh air.

The ground beneath our feet crunched and cracked as we walked towards the vast building before us. It stood out like a blossom in winter against the massive hills that surrounded it. I looked back and noticed that the landing area was not so big and not so far from the edge of the cliff, and gulped in hard. I glanced all around and over the edge and sucked in sharpish at the sight of a sheer drop of swirling mist and cloud. I pulled back my head and focused on the place we were walking to. Ice and a thin covering of snow made our progress fraught with danger and we slipped and stumbled across the narrow, pebble-strewn path that led to the Monastery.

"We do not like this place. We have strange feeling in pit of stomach."

"Do not be afraid, Marcellus, those that abide here are goodly folk and wise."

"Wise enough to give us the info we need?"

"Why else would I bring you here, Adara?" Eadgard said and stopped at a large metal door. It had a slit at eye level that made it look as though it was about to break into a massive grin. "Let me talk for us all."

Eadgard pounded hard upon the door and a glow slithered out from the tiny gash. Then a voice, stern and gruff, spoke, "You are late. Which is inconvenient for the Abbot. Stand back and I will allow you in."

I heard a grinding noise and saw the gigantic door open outwards. A shortish, rotund figure dressed in a black robe that ended at his feet, stood before us. He was without head hair but wore a marvellous grey beard that stretched down to where I assumed his navel would be.

The monk spoke in softish tone. "Follow me and do not say a word. Some of the brothers have taken a vow of silence and must not be engaged in any sort of discourse. This is a place of peace and serenity. Those that abide here do so because they can be assured of privacy. The Abbot, and only he, has access to commune with the outside world. Eadgard, you must relinquish any pods or means of communication gadgets you might have upon your person."

"I have no such instruments."

"I will take you at your word. It is breakfast time here. You will partake of our modest fare? I am Brother Dominic. May the Lord be with you."

"And also with you," Eadgard said and bowed low. "We have come at a direct request, from Abbot Benedict. We are to have an audience with him I believe?"

All in good time. Now, if you will follow me."

CHAPTER 18
Food of the Gods

We entered the building and I almost shouted out
at what I saw - a room so vast that half of all who
lived in Cityplace could have dwelt within it. The
ceiling so high that my eyes could barely focus on the
intricate pics that decorated it. The images were
nothing like I had seen before. They were not photos
or the like, or the pastel doodlings at Wirt's
homeplace. These were soft flowing strokes of colour
and light, depicting all manner of skirmishes and
trouble. I almost went dizzy again from the squinting
up and rubbed my eyes to better focus on the rest of
the fascinating chamber. There were large oblong
windows on both sides that let in a rainbow of light
through their intricate patchwork of coloured glass.

The white walls were indented with alcoves
containing what I took to be brightly painted puppets.
For what purpose their use I could not begin to guess.
Perhaps these religious folk indulged in make believe
and used them for sport? The floor was covered in the
most colourful pelts I had come across. They felt
softer than a kittle-kits fur when I bent low to touch.

Eadgard pulled away my hand and shook his head. I grinned in apology and quickened my step to be in line with Wirt, whose eyes were as wide as a newborn. Marcellus narrowed his and turned his head from side to side as if expecting an attack. I punched his shoulder by way of easing his fear. He rubbed the thwacked spot and I pushed him forward. He moved warily on, glancing at the recesses as though one of the statue things would come to life and pounce upon us all.

We came to a halt by a pair of huge brown wooden doors that made an end to the corridor we had walked down. Brother Dominic held up his hand and nodded towards said entrance.

"We are at the dining room now. Through this portal are many folk. Some are Brothers like myself and some are not. Partake of our humble food, but please, do not engage anyone in talk. You look confused. It is perhaps my choice of wordage. The place we are to enter is a place for the sitting down and consuming of foodstuffs. Do not talk, or should I say, chittle-chat, with any you may find there. Nod if that is clear?" We did and trundled into the place for grub.

The room was brightly lit from long curved pieces of metal all intertwined with each other, with several bent arms jutting out to form a kind of circle. They hung from the ceiling in regular rows and each had a glowing orb stuck in the end of each of its many arms. It was a cheery light that could not but soothe a fretful constitution. Even Marcellus lost the look of suspicion from his face. Clustered in the centre were many tables and chairs, all made from what looked like finest oak wood. I have seen many a pic of furniture such as this in a vid I saw at early school about days of yore. I'd thought they existed only in movie form. I could not wait to touch them and see if they were real.

There were no windows though, which was odd to me. The walls were bare and washed in a soothing pale yellow. On the right hand side was a huge counter filled with many dishes and bowls. Brother Dominic guided us towards it and I smelled a smell so watering of mouth that I nearly dribble-drabbed all down my chin. I could not wait to taste the fresh food that was before me.

"Here, take a plate and choose anything you wish. Do not be afraid, go on, eat. Fill your bowls from as many other bowls as you see fit."

He need not tell us twice. After losing the contents of my gut, and not wanting to remember the stuff we ate in the Clonie Zone, my tum was all but empty and in need of filling. I was first to grab the largest plate I could find and packed it to the brim-full with steaming hot goodies. Wirt, Marcellus and Eadgard followed suit and Brother Dominic, whose plate was scanty compared to ours, showed us to a large table were other similarly attired Monks sat. He gestured for us to plonk our rears and this we did, careful not to lose a single piece of tasty titbits in the speed of our descent. The other Brothers lifted their also bald heads and gave us a welcoming smile. So genuine a look was on their faces that we could not help but to grin right back. When that was done we took our utensils and shovelled in the yummy food. The tastes were such that I felt a drop of wet at the corner of my eyes. Each mouthful caused a happy memory to stir in my confused brain. This nosh was the nosh of a higher place.

When we had finished and licked our plates clean (I say "we" but really it was only Wirt), Brother Dominic pushed his untouched plate forward, leant close and whispered, "Now that you have eaten I must usher you to another area, a place where we can talk in private. For what I need to tell you is not for everyone's ears." He gave a sideways glance and narrowed his eyes as he spoke and a chill spread across the back of my neck. We rose and followed Brother Dominic. I held back for a sec just so that I could pass my hand over the polished wooden tables. Real alright.

The other users looked in our direction as we moved away and I managed to get a quickly glimpse of the assortment of hominids that frequented the area. Mostly Brothers, like Dominic. Some in black robes, some in light brown and some, not Brothers at all. Fems! Dressed like the Brothers only wearing close-fitting soft helmets that covered all their head and neck, so that their faces popped out as though they had stuck their head through a hole in a bedding sheet and forgotten to take it off. I wondered if they too were bald. I nudged Wirt and as discretely as I could manage, pointed at said fems. He looked at them, then at me and bent close to my ear.

"They are the oddliest Ladies I have ever seen. I am dumbstruck with astoundedness to see such here. I had heard that monks had no inkling for the quickie sort of bonk."

"I do not fancy they are fems of that genre. They wear no paint or garments that show off their goodly rations."

"This is a place full to bursting with quiz."

We continued to gawp until we reached the door.
Brother Dominic led us through it. We walked in the
opposite direction to the way we came for a few
steps, and then turned left at a corner and into another
vast corridor also without windows. A gentle light
from glass shells attached to the grey walls made it
look as though the sun would rise at any moment. We
stopped at a black door and he gestured for us to
gather close.

"Are we to see the Abbot now? Is he in here?"

"No, he is not, Adara. That is the Library and is
of no use to you. I brought you here simply because it
is less frequented than other passageways."

"For what purpose?"

"To tell you that you are to become a great
Auger."

"I do not believe in prophecies and the like."

"Perhaps not, but you cannot escape your
destiny."

"Tacky words, Brother. I may gag if you
continue in this manner."

"Indeed, since you do not appreciate my attempts
at clarifying the fate that awaits you all, I will say
only that your mission may take you on a different
path than the one you began."

Well duh-uh! I thought. Big secret. I had
managed to fathom that much myself. What with
being met by a Backpacker and taken to this place in
a flying craft and the like.

"It is true, we are on a journey that has steered
off course a little, but now we are back upon it."
Eadgard said.

"I just wish someone would be direct. To be sure, I have no comprehensions as to who I should trust and who not."

"Adara, those that you think you can trust, may not be so honest. And those that you thought you could not, may be allies after all."

"What? More riddles Eadgard?"

Wirt turned to look at Marcellus, who gave back the glare with the same venom and then some.

"The Abbot Brother, are we to meet?"

"All in good time, Eadgard. First Adara must meet with another."

"Not before the Abbot."

A sound like the falling of many boxes came from the behind the closed door. We turned our attention to said noise and Brother Dominic took my arm.

"Come, Adara."

"Nah. I want to know what made that racket."

"It is nothing."

I pulled myself free and stood in front of the portal. The others joined me and Brother Dominic sighed.

"May you discover all that you require," the monk said and gave us all a glance full of meaning and dread.

I shivered without knowing why and Brother Dominic pulled open the enormous door.

CHAPTER 19
Books!

We stepped into another vast, high-ceilinged room. The air was cold and musty and reminded me of rotting leaves. Not an unpleasant smell at all. In fact, I felt an urge to dwell there, to curl up on the polished wooden floor and have a nap. I wiped my eyes and blinked. I had never seen such a place before. Back home we gained our info by comp or vid and then on a small scale compared to this. It was filled from top to bottom with ancient methods of recording information and make-believe. Rows and rows of wooden ledges bulged to more than their capacity and the floor was all but concealed with books that had fallen from their perch.

"Books. Real and tangible. I had thought it a myth and yarn that such things still abided in our time," I said.

"Books, indeed. All that is left from the last wasteoftime war. I thought only a few remained. This sight overwhelms me indeed. How come there are so many?" Eadgard said.

Brother Dominic smoothed down his long beard, put his hands behind his back and spoke. "Over two hundred years ago, when the Agros first came to power and set about fulfilling their corrupt manifesto, they ordered the destruction of all reading materials. Our dear Brothers saved what they could and hid them until this wondrous place was built. Then brought them here."

"Wow! This has existed for that many orbits?" I said.

"Indeed it has."

"Who built it all?"

"Our very own order of St Anthony of Padua. And before you ask, he is the patron saint of lost things. We engaged people deep with belief in God and the preservation of mankind's past. Of course it helped that they were specialist architects and construction workers. You look disappointed. Did you expect a more spiritual answer?"

"Well, maybe something more obscure."

"Adara, do not pout and spoil that pretty face of yours."

Wirt giggled at the monk's words and I confess to giving over to the pink when Marcellus copped a gander at my whole somewhat stocky frame. I gave the floor a scrutiny until said heat was past and when I lifted my head saw Eadgard smiling fondly at me.

Brother Dominic held out his hand. "Come," he said.

But before I could tell him to go "huff himself," out from behind a stack of books as tall as Marcellus and more, appeared a lady monk like the ones we saw in the place of sitting down. She put her finger to her lips.

"Sshhh. This is a place of serious quiet and contemplation."

Brother Dominic glowered for a sec, resumed his placid look and said, "Ah, sister? Come and greet our most special visitors."

The not quite Lady brushed off her black robe and walked towards us. She cocked her head to one side and screwed up her eyes when she came near to Marcellus. He took a step back as though not at all comfy with such intense scrutiny from a fem that was not a fem.

"This is Sister Gabriel. She is in charge of records. Sorting the books by age and genre. Fact and fiction, that kind of thing."

"All by yerself, ye do this?"

"Yes. I work better alone and faster. I have a method you see," she said to Wirt and stood in front of him. She peered into his eyes like a raptor searching for prey. He looked more than uneasy at her birdle-like stare and tried to cast his glance away. But she moved her body with his eyes; so that wherever he looked she was in focus.

"I had an assistant once, Brother Lance. He works in the sanitation section now. Best place for him. Useless at filing. Put fiction and fact based books on the same shelf. Yes, I work faster and more accurately alone."

"And a sterling job she does too. Already Sister Gabriel has sorted half the books we own, which were in quite a mess before she came," Brother Dominic said and gently guided her away from the nervous Wirt.

Sister Gabriel wriggled free from his grasp and put her hand on her hips. She stuck out her neck and peered at us most rudely.

"Brother, these people are new. Did I hear rightly the name Adara?"

"Indeed you did."

"The one mentioned by the Abbot himself?"

"Yes."

Sister Gabriel rubbed her chin and narrowed her eyes. She moved closer to where we stood and gave Marcellus an intense stare.

"And that one," she said and pointed at said Clonie, "that one is I believe a genetically engineered hominid. I have seen the pictures in scientific journals from the latter part of the twenty-first century. I thought they had all been destroyed. Was it not forbidden to clone a human?"

Sister Gabriel circled Marcellus as she spoke, and as her voice became louder and higher in pitchinesss, he backed away and ended up all squat and scared upon the floor. Brother Dominic stood in between her and Marcellus and raised his hands to prevent her from looming over him.

"Sister, save your questions for a more appropriate occasion. This person deserves as much respect and privacy as anyone here."

"But Brother, if he is a Cl-"

"Sister! Go about your business and leave us to ours."

Sister Gabriel opened her mouth but nowt came out. She took a lasting glance at us all, pursed her lips and disappeared behind another stack of books. Marcellus stood shakily. His big round face was pale and I swear I saw a trickle of moisture slip from the corner of his eye.

"My apologies for Sister Gabriel. She spends all her waking hours in this room. Sometimes I think she reads too much and has lost the ability to relate comfortably with others."

"She is as full-on as a teen on a first date," I said and gave a reassuring grin to Marcellus. This time he went all red and scuffed the floor with his foot.

"Without her considerable help, this archive would have perished. Now Adara, if you will-"

"Come with you to see the Abbot?"

"Well, no. Not just yet."

"Then save your voice. I will linger here until that time."

A gong boomed from somewhere and Brother Dominic turned his head towards the door. He twined his fingers around the ends of his beard and I guessed he was in conflict with what he must do and what I clearly would not.

"That is the bell for prayer. I need to attend the mass. Stay if you must," Brother Dominic said, bowed slightly and left.

CHAPTER 20
Disclosures

Eadgard walked towards me and was about to say something when his words were silenced by Sister Gabriel's voice. "Has he quite gone?"

"Indeed, quite," I said.

Sister Gabriel poked her head around the corner of a pile of books and tapped the side of her small thin nose. "I know things you wish to learn," she said and scooted all quick-quick over to where we stood. "Ask and I will answer."

Eadgard scratched his cheek and said, "Brother Dominic mentioned that this place was in chaos before your arrival. Why so?"

The strange fem coughed most loudly and sent her gaze upwards. We followed suit and clocked the red blip light from several cams, no doubt recording our every word and movement. She "accidentally" knocked over some books, and we all, except for Marcellus, knelt to pick them up. Between the dull thuds of re-stacking, she told us a tale in a hushed voice.

"Before I came here there was a Brother Augustus. He kept things in order. An order that kept some books hidden."

"Why? Ye seem to be all open about their existence."

"Now we are. Now that I'm here. You see, Brother Augustus was not really a man of God," she said and lowered her voice so much so that we all had to bend nearer to her mush to hear what spurted out next. "He was an Agro come to infiltrate our order and discover secrets. Secrets which I cannot divulge to you."

"Huffin' right. Don't seem to want to divulge much of anything," I said and folded my arms. This story, although meaningful I'm certain, was long and meandering and I was bored with it.

"I cannot tell because I do not rightly know. I tell enough. Eyes and ears abound throughout this place. And I would not have them hear what I know. Not everything is as it appears to be," she said and scrunched in next to Eadgard, Wirt and myself. "However, stay this close and I shall draw your attention to this fine illustrated book. Be sure to observe it through eyes that would seem to find its contents of the utmost fascination. You there, large mutant thing, you may come over and listen also." She beckoned to Marcellus. He slow-walked over to us and squatted next to Eadgard. "So, to cut a long story short-"

"Finally," I said and as one we huddled around the tome with pics and worldles in that I could not read.

"To cut a long story short, especially for Adara, he wanted access to the science books we keep for those who have the understanding and knowledge to decipher them. He spent long hours searching; rifling through our archive and rearranging the order they were in. I, who was new here, noticed the books were all messed up and one day caught the Brother breaking into the secret vault. When I accosted him he turned most savage, but I was able to stave off his violent attack. I sat upon his chest and screamed until help arrived. He was taken away and I was given the task of undoing the damage he had done."

Eadgard looked at the sister and gave her a nod as if to suggest he was impressed. "There is more to you than meets the eye, Sister, truly I do think so."

"The same could be said of you."

"What?"

Sister Gabriel tilted her head to one side, and then flicked Eadgard on the forehead. "Do not be coy, S.A.N.T. You too have much to tell Adara, and the others I think?"

Eadgard huffed and puffed and scratched the back of his neck. Sister Gabriel folded her arms, "Speak then. You know of what."

"I do?"

"Think. Shake off the muddlehead caused by too much munchings. Come let us go to a more secluded spot downwind of these cams and their mics. I know they cannot pick up words said in softness," Sister Gabriel said and waved her arms at the ceiling, where we saw many lenses hanging down from it.

We stood and I began to wobble as if I were about to keel over. Eadgard put his arms around me and supported my shaky back. Sister Gabriel pointed to a table and chairs that were partly hidden behind a wall of books. We all plodded to the place and sat down heavily.

Sister Gabriel leant low across the table and said, "Say what you must."

Eadgard took in a goodly breath, exhaled loudly and belched. "I shall begin. Adara, please do not become alarmed by what I have to say."

I looked to Wirt. His head was drooped forward and he blinked-blinked often, suggesting a struggle with consciousness. Marcellus nudged him and he raised his noggin.

Eadgard cleared his throat and kept-on. "Your meeting with the Nearlymen. It was your Santy who told the guards to send you near to their camp. She needed you to meet with Wirt and for him to take you to the Ladies so that they could deliver you to me."

"Wait a sec, I have never met ye or yer kind. How ye know me and my link with the Ladies?"

"There are those amongst your kin that play a vital role in the plan we are all involved in."

"What? We are part of grand design?"

"Well, no Marcellus, you were not a part of the grand scheme of things."

"However, I have a feeling he is now bound up in your destiny," said Sister Gabriel and both Marcellus and myself exchanged a red-tinged look.

"What? That near savage creation? What are ye talking of? Nonsense and bunkum. Do not listen to 'em, Adara. They are spinning ye a yarn as long as a grand old river."

"No Wirt, no yarn. All that I tell is the truth. There is a plot brewing, a scheme to infiltrate the Agros," Eadgard said.

"Audrey hinted as much."

Sister Gabriel chewed on her lip and gave me one of her intense stares. "You are as yet unpolished. Therefore, ill-equipped to continue your journey to a successful end."

"I concur with Sister Gabriel. Part of my mission is to make sure you are at your full potential before carrying on," Eadgard said.

"What? What potential? This is new," I said. Sister Gabriel put a finger to her lips and I lowered my voice. "Time is all a-pressing is it not? My bro-bro cannot wait for me to come into my prime, whatever that is."

"Rest, rest, Adara. You will meet again with your brother."

"When? Where?"

Sister Gabriel tapped her nose. "Ah, now, that would be telling."

I slapped my thighs. "Here we go again. I must say that I am more than weary of all this deviousness and intrigue," I said and rose from the table. I walked away and plonked myself all sulky upon a small pile of books. Sister Gabriel stood abruptly and raised her voice so all could hear.

"Ahhhh! Get your greatly arse off those treasured tomes," she said, and waved her hands about as though chasing away a buzzy thing. Eadgard, Wirt and Marcellus jumped up from their chairs. Sister Gabriel lurched towards me with a look of mean upon her face. I was overcome with confusion as to her actions, when over her shoulder I saw Brother Dominic enter carrying a small tray of delicious food. I wondered then if she contrived her freakish manner for his benefit.

"Off! Off I say, you lump!"

"Fine and dandy, Sister. This I'll do without your need to carry on so," I said and walked past her to the table. I wide-eyed my friends and they shrugged, then we all sat down. Brother Dominic placed the tray of food before us. The fresh slivers of fruit and sweet cakes seemed to speak to my stomach and without a second thought I, Eadgard, Wirt and Marcellus grabbed said morsels and gobbled them up.

Brother Dominic turned to Sister Gabriel and said, "Will you partake of a snack?"

"No, no, later. No time for munching."

"As you will, Sister. But please do eat something. Your lack of appetite has not gone unnoticed."

"We fear no such thing occur for self or friends," Marcellus said and wiped his mouth on his sleeve.

I gulped down what I was eating and sat back. Wirt yawned, folded his arms and let his head nod forward. Eadgard ceased his guzzling and blinked. He stared into space for a few secs, looked down and tapped his fingers on the table. "We were discussing things. I was about to tell of your purpose."

Sister Gabriel coughed most loudly. Behind Brother Dominic's back, she pointed to the ceiling cams. The monk turned swiftly and the sister used her locating finger to rub her eye. Eadgard, oblivious to all this subterfuge, continued on. "Adara, you must use your voice-"

Eadgard's words shook my innards and sent a wave of fire throughout my bod. Not the catcher of birds stuff again. Something snapped and I let rip. "Nah! No, naddar I won't. I am not a puppet for you to yank on every time you want some meat. I thought up here that such greedy mindedness would be impossible, but I was wrong. You are all the same.

All you care about is meat, filthy, huffin' meat!" I
fairly shrieked and stood.

The chair that I was plonked on skittered across
the floor sending books flying this way and that.
Sister Gabriel pursed her lips and went to pick up the
books that I had scattered. Wirt, good solid Wirt,
came and wrapped his arms around my waist.

"No, you misunderstand me, Adara," Eadgard
said. He rose slowly from the table, wobbled for a sec
then walked over to where I stood with Wirt. "No one
here wants you to call the birds for food."

I felt Wirt tighten his grip upon me and was glad
of his reassurance.

"I'll not leave yer side, Adara."

"I hope you never will, Wirt. We are, according
to Eadgard, bound together anyhoo."

Eadgard lowered his gaze, and then looked at me
all-serious-like.

"I brought you here because the Abbot wished it
so. I was to take you to a safe location just beyond the
Beyondness boundaries. But I learned of these new
instructions when I used the com device at the Clonie
camp. For what purpose you are here, I cannot tell."

"Ah, but I can," Brother Dominic said and joined
us. "Eadgard is right. The Abbot wanted you here to
see a monk, Brother Jude, who has been waiting for
you all of his years, which are many. This brother is
to school you in how to use your voice to reach its
full potential. He is the person I was eager for you to
see."

I pulled away from Wirt, folded my arms across
my chest and gave Eadgard and the Brother a
suspicious look. "For what purpose?"

"For the singing of the song that makes all things disremember," Brother Dominic said.

I pushed my face close to the monk, "And what has that to do with finding my bro?"

"The Abbott, and only he, can give you that most portentous answer."

I stared into his blank eyes. The monk smiled a most suspicious smile and I looked to the others. All but Sister Gabriel stared at Brother Dominic as though he were the keeper of all knowledge. I stepped back and felt a wooziness sweep over me. I took in some breaths and the dullness waned.

"Rightly fine. And when he does, we can continue our mission."

"In time. Brother Jude is waiting."

Brother Dominic stood so rigid and firm of purpose that I utterly failed to suggest that I go to the Abbot right quickly. I simply said, "Right, fine and how long will I need to be with this monk?"

"Oh, I cannot say, but it may be a while."

A sigh from Marcellus filled the room and both he and Wirt snorted in derision.

Wirt folded his arms and wobbled his head as if he were about to blub. "And what are we to do whilst she is so occupied?"

Brother Dominic waved his arm in a massive arc around the room. "Wirt, you are in a library. The only one left in all of NotsoGreatBritAlbion. I would have thought that you and Marcellus could quite easily busy yourselves for many moons with the reading of these rare tomes."

Wirt looked down. "Ye being funny or what?"

"I do not have much capacity for jest. I am a monk of an order that relishes thought and contemplation. Frivolities are for those who have less time or inclination for matters of importance."

"I did not glean so much from what ye just said there Brother, but if ye are not jesting then ye must be thick."

"I am no such thing, young man."

"I am a Forestdweller. I have not done so much in the way of reading. Not sure if the Clonie over there has either."

"We do not look at words, we speak and tell," Marcellus said and got up from the table. He ambled over to Eadgard and put his hands behind his back.

Brother Dominic scratched his head and blinked once or twice. "We have books with pictures. Lots of them in fact. I'm sure Sister Gabriel will be happy to show you where they are."

"We not comfortable with notion of spending time with said Sister."

"Granted, Marcellus, Sister Gabriel reacted to your presence with unusual enmity. However, I believe it was the shock of seeing a creature she thought extinct."

"All same, we not happy," Marcellus said.

"I will stay and gladly keep you company," Eadgard said and led Marcellus back to the table.

"Aye, me too. I am all a-weary anyhow," Wirt said and joined them.

"A good idea, Eadgard. Now, Adara, please come with me."

I did not know why I felt compelled to do the Brother's bidding, but something dull seemed to sit inside my head. So heavily that all thoughts of what I was and what I should be doing, drifted away. I nodded to the others and gave a shrug as if to suggest my compliance in what was to occur, and followed Brother Dominic towards the exit.

I stopped at the door and took one last look back. I saw Sister Gabriel stagger towards Wirt, Marcellus and Eadgard with a whole pile of thick books in her arms. They yawned and slumped back into their chairs, elbows on the table and fists propping up their weary heads. My heart flip-flopped all quickly and I gasped quite breathless for a sec. Then whatever it was that caused such anxiousness disappeared. I turned away, stepped into the corridor and shuffled after Brother Dominic, not knowing what was to come next.

CHAPTER 21
Brother Jude

We turned down another wide passageway made up of small uneven bricks that were grey and dull, and gave the place a gloomy tone. Half way down we stopped by a dark recess in the wall. Brother Dominic stepped into it and gestured for me to follow. I did and saw a narrow staircase made from the same lumpy stone. It twisted up and round and try as I might I could not see an end to it.

"At the top of these stairs is a room. It will be the place where you will reside during your stay with us. It is also the room that Brother Jude abides."

"What? I'm to linger in the same spot with an oldie? Nah, this is wrong and somewhat sordid."

"Not so. Let me put your mind at rest by reassuring you of Brother Jude's advancing years and his vow of celibacy. He will not be a threat to your maidenhood. He is your mentor and guide to achieving your true potential. You must listen and act on his teachings."

"Some of what you said filtered through and I am a little reassured. Eadgard and sister Gabriel made much of my inexperience. It maybe goodly to partake of learning to better my chances of finding my bro. I'll be allowed some rec time? To see Wirt and the rest?"

"Of course. You will take your meals in the dining room with the rest of us."

"The place of sitting down?"

"Exactly. Now, please, follow me."

I wriggled my shoulders and felt the reassuring thud of my Synthbag against them. All thoughts about the other thingy that I thought I needed to do vanished. My mind focused on the unsavoury notion that I must dwell with a near-dead 'dult. I was somewhat feared at meeting Brother Jude, never having really got up close to a wrinkleyone before, except for greatgrangran. All the ancient hominids in Cityplace went to linger as one group, put away from the rest when they reached a goodly age. We saw them on special occasions, then mostly from afar when they trundled around the so-called "One-and-only-Park."

I followed Brother Dominic onto the staircase, which became narrower the higher we climbed. And though I am trained and toned, I found the ascent stressful upon the lungs and breathed heavily and loud. Brother Dominic seemed not to take in air and flittered up the steps as if they weren't there at all. I marvelled at his vigour, seeing that he too could be deemed as old.

Just when I thought that I might topple from lack of oxygen, Brother Dominic came to a halt. He stopped by a wide flat area illuminated by a patterned glass window. The light streamed through it and made little coloured blocks of red and blue stick to the wall and floor like un-curved rainbows. It also lit up a dark brown door behind the Monk.

"We are here. As you can see there are no other rooms but this one. No one comes here so you will not be disturbed. Now I must leave you. You must enter alone," he said and walked past me.

"Oy, no wait a sec. I cannot go in solo."

"You will. You must. It is the way of things," he said, turned and walked down the spiral staircase. I called his name but he did not answer. I folded my arms and stared at the bars of colour that changed shape before my eyes, and wondered what to do. Then I heard an unfamiliar sound come from Brother Jude's room. It was a high, thin warbley noise like something a raptor chickle might make if it was sickly. It changed to a low, low growl and despite my uneasiness I stepped closer to its source.

From behind the imposing door a nasal whine floated out. It was the darndest thing I had ever heard. It seemed to slip into my ear holes as delicately as a wisp of summer wind and I could not help but press my lobe against the dark wood to better hear.

I did not get the chance to eavesdrop further, as said door was pulled sharply open. I saw nought but blur and ended up all splattered face down onto a soft pelt. After spittle-spatting out some ancient fluff, I gathered together my surprised senses and stood.

Before me was a tall, thinly ancient. His eyes were large and the palest blue I had ever seen. Unlike the other monks that I saw, he had a thick head of white hair that hung down to his shoulders. His face was smooth. I had expected many lines and wrinkles. But despite the lack of crevices, he had an air of age about him and smelt of burning wood. His nose was as large and similar in shape to the beak of an eagle, and his lips were full and red.

"Adara, welcome," he said in a voice as sweet as honey. So sweet and rich in friendship that I gave myself up to cheer and held out my hand just like that. He took it and clasped his fingers around mine. His grip was strong for one so rich in time passing and I squeezed back, not wanting him to let go.

"Yes, for sure you are the one. She with six instead of five. She with hair the colour of ripe corn and eyes the colour of a winter sky. She that can save herself from danger of assault. Adara, the catcher of birds. Adara, the singer of dreams to come," he said and dropped my hand.

"S'pose so," I said, all lame, and felt a familiar heat flush up my neck and cheeks.

"Do not be awkward with who you are. We are all to play a part in what is to come. Granted, your role will be pivotal, but all who stay with you will have a function meaningful. Ah, my girl, how long I have waited for you. I am all skittish as if a boy again. Come let us sit and unbend before the work begins."

He took my am and led me to a grand wooden chair with a high back carved in animal shapes. I sat upon the red cushion and felt my backside sigh at the softness of it all. I let my weary upper limbs slump upon the arms of the chair and leant back. Brother Jude pulled a similar seat to face me and also sat. He put his elbows on his knees, rested his chin on his cupped hands and grinned.

"I will need to hear what you can do before we begin your training. So, if you would be so kind as to go to that far window, open it and call forth a raptor or two, I will be able to assess your ability and tailor your classes accordingly."

I bit my lip and let a look of worry spread across my brow. Brother Jude sat back and stared hard into my eyes. Then without another word, he stood, went to the window that was made up of criss-cross diamond shapes, and opened it.

He leant out and I heard a high-pitched shrill sound. "Eagle, I think and quite near. Come, try it. Call to this creature."

I stood and went to the window. Brother Jude stepped aside and I put my head out. I saw snow-capped tips of mountains in the distance. Clouds swirled around them like ghosties at play and I felt a shiver pass through my innards. The air was cold and clean and I closed my eyes and filled my lungs with its purity.

"Sing, Adara. Call its name, its true name, and it will come."

"What? I don't know what birds call themselves."

"Then listen and it will tell you."

I stretched my neck out farther, squeezed my eyes shut tighter, and focused my hearing on the screams and shrill notes that floated around my head. I listened intently, and to my surprise, thought I heard a name of sorts. I opened my mouth and sang the note that best resembled the one I heard. In no more than the passing of a breath, I earholed the shriek of a large raptor. I pulled back from the window and in flew a golden eagle. It flapped and flopped around the room leaving large brown striped feathers on the floor. I shielded my face with my hands lest it decided to munch upon some fresh meat.

"Soothe it, quickly."

"How?"

"Lower your voice to the tenderest of a sound."

I did so and made a "Coo, coo" noise almost in a whisper. The bird ceased its panic and came to rest upon the arm of Brother Jude's chair.

"There, my friend. No need to fear," he said, walked over to it and to my gasps, began to stroke its head. The creature half closed its eyes and ruffled up its feathers before settling down to a snooze.

"Brother Jude, that was impressivo in the extreme. How came I to tame such a wild and dangerous thing?"

"This bird is not tame. You have merely caused it forget its fear of humans. You have caused it to believe that it is among friends who will do it no harm. You have also added a note or two that has made it forget what tasty morsels we are."

"How did I do that?"

"By listening to its heart. You must have done something similar before?

"I have, a little. I called upon a chikle to return to-" I stopped before I blabbed about the Lady camp.

"Ah, I knew it."

"How long will it stay?" I said by way of diverting his thoughts from what I almost revealed.

"Until you sing another tune to make it want to flee."

"I cannot do such a thing. I can only make them gather and do the thing they do. Which is tear and rip and nosh upon flesh."

"But you have."

"Well, nah. Not really. The chickle wanted to return. My name dictates what I must do and that is to catch I guess and not to change their minds."

"Your name guides. It is you who dictates how you use your power."

I dared to approach the bird and Brother Jude gestured for me to put my hand upon its head. I did with more than a little trepidation. It angled its head so that I could scratch underneath its chin. I was filled with the same pleasure and tender-feel as when I stroked the kittle for the first time. I turned to the ancient monk and saw a look of rapture upon his face.

I let my hand fall to my side and said, "What was your given?"

"Alawn."

"The bringer of melody. The singer of joy."

"Indeed."

"You sang for many and made them all happy?"

"No. At first all I could do was make people sleep with my song. Then I received a calling from the one True God and the path that I must follow. All I learned came from far away, a high and holy place called Tibet."

"I have seen vids of the place. The monks wear orange and do the dandiest chants. But they do not follow the Babychesus."

"No, but they follow a similar doctrine of peace and love to all. And they possess the strongest of powers. They taught me well and now it is time to pass on what I can to you."

"I am willing and ready," I said.

"Then we must begin. Send the eagle home. Try a low sound, from the belly."

I took in a huge breath and let forth a low guttural tone that sent the birdie whisking through the still open window and out into the fading light.

He shut said portal, stood opposite me, closed his eyes and took a breath so deep that I thought he would explode. Then he parted his lips ever so slightly and let out a low-pitched bass sound that burrowed into my body. I felt it resonate throughout my insides and skull, so much so that I began to quiver. He made the noise louder and deeper and I became aware of air between my feet and the floor below me. I peered down and saw that I was floating some ways from the ground. Now, normally I would be all set to barf from the motion of it all and dizzy from the height, but his voice was so strong and secure that I gladdened to be defying gravity with such ease. I let myself succumb to the lack of ground and felt a tingle inside and out. All nausea and fright melted away and I near burst with the thrill of it. He slowly raised the pitch and I descended. My legs wobbled for a sec then I stood straight and tall, a grin spread right across my mush.

"Catcher of birds must learn what it feels like to fly in order to know how to control the soaring of those with wings. Raptors are the most difficult to control."

"Yep, this I know." An image of the Manlymen and Nearlys all huddled and bloodied filled my head. I lowered my gaze and said, "I have made raptors do my bidding and hurt those that had offended a dear one."

Brother Jude's face darkened. He took a step or two towards me and gripped my shoulders. I felt his fingers come into contact with my Synthbag and yank it from my arm.

"Oy. That is mine, that is not for anyone else but me," I said and pulled myself free. I squatted down to pick up my most precious, but Brother Jude kicked it so hard that it skidded across the stone floor and underneath a black table with drawers.

"You will not resort to tech whilst you are here. Brother Dominic should have told you. As for your confession about the raptors, consider my confiscation of your luxuries to be a punishment. This I will say but once. You never use your power to inflict harm. You have not been correctly schooled, so from this day you will hear what I say and do as I teach."

I was red with rage. No one touches my Synthbag and gets away with it. I did not hear much of what he blabbed, so vexed was I with his actions. Without ponder, I opened my mouth and out came a filthy husky sound. I threw it at him as though it was a solid thing and he flopped onto the floor. I stopped all abrupt when I gandered what I had done. He lay as still as a fallen twig and I clasped my hands to my mouth.

"Impressive. I shall enjoy coaching you, little missile," he said and held his hand out for me to take. "A little help, if you please."

I pulled him up and he dusted off his robe. I could not look him in the face and hung my head in shame. "Come, now that you have had your tantrum I believe we can begin our first lesson."

"I am not worthy."

"On the contrary, you have shown me passion and pluck and remorse. Traits vital in order to become greater than you are. If you are willing we will begin with how to breathe."

"Wha"? But I know how to do that."

"Not really. Come, you must learn to suck deep and keep the air inside for more than you can bear, then let it out in controlled gasps. Do as I do and try not to faint."

He placed my hands upon my ribs and told me to take a breath. I did and he set about aiding me in how to keep it in and how to let it out so that I could manipulate its force. A mechanical and simple thing that was anything but easy to achieve. I had to suck through my nose whilst blowing through my mouth, and vice versa, all at the same time.

After many failed attempts and what seemed like four moon passings, I made some progress. The dizziness and dryness of mouth lessened and I was apt enough in its execution to make a soothing song for longer than it took to walk the corridor and climb the stairs to this chamber. And all done in one great breath. So caught up in my exercises was I, that I did not notice night had fallen.

"What is next?"

"Patience, little missile. Enough for today," Brother Jude said and lit some big candles on his desk.

"Enough? But-"

"The hours have sped. Look, it is quite dark and time for you to eat."

"So riveted was I in all this discipline that I have forgot the rumblings that jumbled in my belly."

"Go now and see your friends. I'm sure they will be glad of your company."

"Will you not partake and join us all? I have a strong desire for you and them to make acquaintance."

"I am a solitary soul and do not find the company of others to my liking. I remain here and Brother Dominic brings food."

"Shame it is though. I know Wirt would be impressed."

"Perhaps soon you can invite him here."

"Greatly news, I would relish the act," I said and opened the door.

"Stay as long as you wish. I shall be asleep when you return. Remain quiet and slumber in the chamber behind the arras," he said and pointed to a long embroidered pelt that hung from the ceiling. "My bed is there. As you can see it is far enough away from yours. Fear not."

"I won't. Sleep well, Brother Jude," I said and left.

CHAPTER 22
Know Who Your Friends Are

I skipped down the stone stairway and through the long corridor to the place of sitting down, or the dining room, as it was known. I paused by the entrance and searched the room for Wirt and the others. At the far end, sitting at a great table, were my companions, and Sister Gabriel. She was gesticulating in an impressive fashion and all but Marcellus was attending to her every word. He sat head down, supping from a bowl. I marched quickly over, all eager to relate my experiences with Brother Jude.

My progress was halted by the most scrummy smell. It was hard to describe because I had never smelt the like before. If pressed, I should say that it reminded me of spring and summer when the wind brings the scent of possibility and growth. My belly yelled to be filled and I followed my nose to a counter laid with the most delicious food. I threw all manner of tasties onto a plate and hurried over to where the others sat.

"Adara, welcome. Come sit and feast with us," Eadgard said and down I plunked. Sister Gabriel turned her head towards mine and sighed.

"Ah, I can tell by the glow upon your cheeks that you have partaken of a rare experience. I too had such a look the first time I felt the presence of the one True God. I am pleased for you."

She placed her soft hand upon mine and patted it. I smiled, pulled away and set about reducing the grub on my plate to nothing.

"Adara, what happened to ye up there in the abode of the mystifying monk?"

I swallowed the last remaining morsel and replied. "Wirt, I learnt to fly."

"Metaphorically speaking I suppose," Eadgard said.

"Nope, I left the ground and hovered. Brother Jude made it so. Then he schooled me in how to make my breath last for longer than any can imagine." I had hoped for some expression of wonderment from my friends, but all they did was stare at my countenance with a look of dumb.

"Sister Gabriel has recounted such yarns. She has entertained us so that we did not yearn for ye as much as we ought."

I confess to feeling glum at Wirt's remark. I wanted them to be all impressed and eager to hear more. I sensed from the sound of munching that was not to be the case, so I gulped down a veg and said, "Glad to hear such news. I will be gone for longer still and it is goodly to know that you be with someone who can make the moon and sun's passing go with speed."

Sister Gabriel, who was not eating, looked around at the others and their disinterest in all things concerning me, and said, by way of placating my look of peeve, "Come tell us more."

"I would not weary you with the reciting of it?"

"Not one bit."

Sister Gabriel nudged Wirt's elbow and he dropped the food that was on his fork. He looked at me and then at her. "Aye, I would have ye tell and then some."

"So would I, my dear. Brother Jude is elusive and so conjures up much speculation. I know some things, but would know extra of the man."

"And you Marcellus? Would you revel in the telling of my tale?"

Marcellus had not moved all the time we spoke. He swirled his spoon around a bowl of something that must once have held a tasty hot broth. At my words he dropped the metal scoop and sent some of its contents splurting across the table. He raised his head and stared into my eyes.

"If you want tell story, tell. We care not much. We care about journey which you appear to forget."

"What journey?"

"The one you do not recall."

Something stirred in my noggin. My bro-bro's face appeared for a sec then vanished. "I do recall, Marcellus, I do. Neither I, nor the others have forgot. It's just that, well... Brother Dominic has explained why we are to linger."

"We do not wait in ease like rest. We itch to be gone. We trust no one," Marcellus said and looked at Sister Gabriel who returned his gaze with a raised eyebrow.

"I think we all wish to assume our mission, but as Adara has said, we must wait until the time is proper."

"We will do so, Eadgard, but not with gladness."

I could not help but notice how intensely Sister Gabriel stared at Marcellus and gleaned how twitchy it must make him.

"Sister, if I may make an inquiry?"

"Ask me anything, Adara."

"Why is that you pursue Marcellus so?"

"Do I?"

"Most assuredly so."

"Then I do it without conscious knowledge."

"Then we would sooner not have gaze."

"I am a curious person by nature and merely without malice I assure, have peeked. A natural reaction to an oddity."

"We are not considered odd amongst our own."

"Well said, good Marcellus. Let that be an end to any discomfort caused by the spirit of inquiry," Eadgard said.

Sister Gabriel gave a lopsided grin and positioned her large green eyes at Wirt.

"Ye can cease yer glarings in my direction too. I have a liking for ye but that may pale if ye continue scrutinising so."

"My, my, I have never met with such sensitive males. I may have to go about in blinkers from now on so as to not offend your delicate feelings."

Sister Gabriel stood and folded her arms. I heard her making a clicking noise with her tongue before nodding her head three times. "So this is the state of things. I will speak only when spoken to from now on, and if you require certain knowledge's that only I possess, then you may come to me. I shall not seek you out. Goodnight and may the Lord be with you."

"And also with you," Eadgard said and nodded his head in her direction.

"Oh yeah, and also with you," I said closely followed by Wirt but not Marcellus.

"Will you not bid me a simple goodnight?"

Marcellus looked at Sister Gabriel. He made a sigh then said, "Also with you."

Eadgard pushed his plate away, slapped his tum and yawned. "I am weary for sure. As you all look to be."

"Brother Dominic has prepared a dorm for the three of you to share," Sister Gabriel said and both Wirt and Marcellus frowned.

"Do not make such faces. Our weariness will outweigh any misgivings we have about sharing the same place," Eadgard said.

"Well, if you are ready to take rest then follow me," Sister Gabriel said. "If not, the room is at the end of the first corridor you met when you entered, through a recess and on the right. There is a name upon the door; Saint Francis. You should be able to find it well."

"I shall follow willingly."

"Good, Eadgard. Wirt?"

"I will abide longer and chat with Adara."

"And you Marcellus?"

"We will stay."

"Then I shall see you all when the sun rises, if you wish it."

"Goodnight to you all," Eadgard said and left with Sister Gabriel.

There was a lack of conversation for what seemed an endless period. Then Wirt took a great sigh and put his hands behind his head.

"What a passage of time we have undertaken. I cannot quite focus on the details of the things I have seen and done and… Eaten."

Marcellus slapped the table and let rip a loudly guffaw. Wirt and I did too and I felt the tension-filled air, lift. Wirt wiped the tears from his eyes and took my hand. I was glad to feel his tender grip and could not help but smile at his wordless comfort. Marcellus coughed and I turned to face him.

"Your mood has lightened since the departure of Sister Gabriel."

"It has. We have feeling she not as good as she would make us believe."

"Why do you say such a thing?" I said. "She has been more than civil to us. Maybe a little rudely towards yourself, but methinks it is because she finds you so fascinating."

"Not sure if true. We be careful of such scrutiny. We must not be found out."

"But you are with us on this journey. Others will see you."

"True, but won't be of consequence. We at war with enemy. Matters little if they see face before die."

"Marcellus, ye bring us down to reality with yer words. We are at war for sure and must not be diverted from our goal."

"We not sure of Wirt, now we certain. He solid, he true, he trustworthy above all."

"Do you consider me to be one of honour too?" I asked.

"Will see. Used to, not much now. Singing? What purpose?"

"This I am doubtful on. I used to know, or thought I did, but after my time with Brother Jude, I am thinking there is a plan afoot and that I am to be more than a part of it. So do you, I believe."

"Careful not to forget mission. Careful to stay true. Careful to stay as are and not as others want to make you."

"Adara is true and good and brave and would never give us cause to think otherwise," Wirt said and squeezed my hand. I squeezed back not greatly certain that I could live up to Wirt's kind words. A fuzziness spread throughout my body and I let go of Wirt's hand. He let it flop at his side and let out a sigh. Marcellus yawned and I did too, then we all smiled. I struggled to stand, so fatigued I was and needed to pat my cheeks to clear my head.

"It is late, so late. I must to bed dear Wirt and Marcellus. Sleep sound and happy both," I said and left them to wander to their own place of lying down.

The corridor was not as well lit as before. The brightness was replaced with an amber glow that was not at all displeasing. It made a mood of serenity creep through me and I began to understand the appeal of this higher than high-up place. There was no sound at all except the soft padding of my feet upon the stone floor and I stopped to stare at a pelt hanging on the wall. It was made from woven straw and had coloured shapes streaked through it. At first I thought they were all-random but on closer inspection became aware that they depicted a strange and gruesome scene.

"The stations of the cross."

I jumped at the sound of Sister Gabriel's voice. It cut through the stillness like a raptor screech at the dead of night. She placed her hand upon my shoulder and I felt her grip tighten. "There are more of these on each wall. They tell the story of the Babychesus all grown and condemned to death. There is great beauty amongst this tragic tale."

"Um, yep if you so say, Sister."

"You cannot see it because you are not initiated in our great faith. You Citydwellers believe in only tech and being clean. I have seen, I have witnessed. There is more to life than making newones and scrubbing floors."

"Duh-uh, I know."

"Do you, Adara?"

"I am here and not getting ready to tie-the-knot as I am expected at my coming-of-age. So, yeah, I know."

"Perhaps. I shall walk you to your destination and have a friendly chat."

She let go of my shoulder and slid her arm through mine. We walked towards my place of rest as slow as an ancient 'dult trying to scrabble up an incline. I tried to lean away from her pressing in, but to my surprise, she was stronger than she looked and had me firmly secured against her side.

"I left young Eadgard by his quarters and returned stealth-like back to the dining area where I spied and listened in on your ramblings. Do not think me bad for this. I did so as to hear the truth of things from lips that would not open so honest whilst I remained. Marcellus is correct in his warnings to you. This place is godly and divine alright, but has other things that press upon it beyond the call of God. I will caution you, as did Marcellus. Learn from Brother Jude by all means, but do not believe or do only-onto-him. I am of late become suspicious of this and that. When you arrived I realised my fancy had substance."

"Explain more."

"I cannot just yet my dear. Know this though, I have not seen or heard the Abbot for more than eight days."

I opened my mouth to seek more info, but Sister Gabriel halted before the stone stairway that led to Brother Jude's room.

"We are here. Rest and be wary. I am a friend. Believe that much," she said, released my arm and scuttled quick as a beetle down the corridor and out of sight.

CHAPTER 23
A Letting-Go of All Things Learned

I entered the darkened chamber and spied Brother Jude in bed. He lay flat upon his back, a thick woollen blanket pulled up against his chin. It was red and blue and fatter than any pelt I had seen. I wondered at how he procured such a prize, wool being the most pricey of materials. All my coverings came from a lab. Processed and squished until out pops material to make all manner of coverings for bed, floor, wall and bod. The mystery of this man and place became all the more intense. I tippy-toed past his closed eyes, pulled aside the thick hanging and entered the place I was to rest in.

It was sparse and no mistake, with just a single chair and slim wooden bed pushed against the far wall. Above it was a plain glass window shaded with a heavy red drape. I looked around for a place to hang my clothes and saw a rod sticking out from the opposite wall with large hooks hanging from it.

My ballooned belly gurgled. I searched for a special place to relieve myself and noticed a plain screen made of wooden slats opposite my bed and glanced behind. I saw a pissing pot with a pipe attached that went out through the wall. And to my great happiness, a shower. That was when I remembered my stricken Synthbag in the Monk's room. I needed it for my 'blutions for sure. So I sidled back in and crawled along the floor until I spied it under a table. I stretched my arm out and pulled it to my chest. Then I pid-padded all quiet-like back to my own quarters and sploshed and plopped until I felt all-clean.

Dry and warmed through, I ambled towards the bed and clambered in. Sleep was not forthcoming due to Sister Gabriel's words. I tossed and turned and thought about what she said for a bit, then nestled into the small yet comforting mattress. I shut my lids, let the blackness soothe my questioning brain, and fell asleep.

I thought that I'd just nodded off and not slept the sleep of profundity, since no dreams appeared to make all sense of things that passed. I opened my eyes and saw Brother Jude swish aside the curtains to let the daylight flood throughout my unlit chamber. His brown robe brushed against my blinking awake face and I opened my mouth as wide as an owlet downing some meat and let out a back-throat yawn.

"Light so soon?"

"Always the sun rises when it should. I would have you refreshed and ready. First partake of breakfast. Pardon me, perhaps you refer to it as 'first-of-day-food?'"

"Now and then, when chatting with family folk and the like. I wonder, Brother Jude, if I might bring forth grub for you to chew upon?"

"Kindly gesture, but I have a reliable source that has already fed and watered my every need for nourishment. I rise before the sky gets light."

"Perhaps later?"

"No, use the eating times to keep a closeness with your companions. Now rise and eat and return for your next lesson," he said and left me to dress. I only had one clean garment at the bottom of my Synthbag. A long black skirt made from non-nano thread. It felt all heavy and clingy against my legs. The top as well, so when I put all on, I felt as though I had got into another's skin. Shaking off the unpleasant sensation, I hitched on my Synthbag, left my resting place and entered Brother Jude's chamber. He was leaning out of the window taking in a big lungful of air. He turned and smiled and waved his hands in a gesture meaning "go". I shuffled out and ran all the way to the dining room.

It was full of the hominids we had seen the day before and I noticed that some 'dult males wore the same kind of plaid skirt that Wirt and his kin wore. I spied my companions standing at the food area and sped keenly towards them. The smell of warm grub and hot beverages filled my senses to capacity and I quite forgot what I was thinking for a time. Eadgard was the first to greet me by a hardy slap on my shoulder, followed by a huggle from Wirt and a serious nod from Marcellus. I was about to blab about Sister Gabriel's cryptic chittle-chat when I saw her approach.

"A new day. Praise the Lord. All still alive and well and engaging in a healthy appetite."

"The grub is the best I have ever eaten for sure."

"I suppose it is, Adara. City food is mostly processed and lacks the flavour and texture of the real thing."

"I was non the wiser as to such foodstuffs before I began this adventure. Now that I have tasted such wonders I do not think I can return to the consuming of my previous synthetic fare."

"I pray you never need to."

"We are curious as to meaning in that phrase."

"No meaning, Marcellus, I merely desire young Adara to always eat the most delicious of food."

"Not possible when we continue mission. Must needs eat reconstituted and processed grub. No access to fresh."

"Quite so, Marcellus, quite so. Pardon my error. Perhaps though, you might wish to eat less of this fine cuisine and begin to acclimatise yourselves to the more bland foodstuffs that you will be feeding on when you do resume your quest."

"I think not, Sister," I said and snorted in the scrumptious aromas. "The day will be long and full, I must fuel my bod to get through it all."

"More of same for us too. We become weary of it. Your absence, Adara, we notice much."

"Do not be fraught, Marcellus. You shall not miss Adara. I will show you books to engage your mind and set your curiosity to tumble and twist," Sister Gabriel said.

"You have piqued my interest at least, good Sister. I am sure Wirt and Marcellus will thrill to your revealings also."

"They will to be sure. Now I must go and select tomes of curiosity whilst you chitchat and catch up. Perhaps, Adara, we will enjoy your company at some juncture. There is a book, which may prove most enlightening, and I would wish you to share its wisdom. Perhaps at mid-morning prayers, which Brother Jude must needs to undertake, you may slip away and join your friends in the library?"

"You intrigue me greatly and I shall be there."

"Good, good. Until later all," she said and left at a most rapid pace.

We piled our plates and sat opposite a group of plainly dressed folk and set to gobble up our break of fasting. I noticed that the other hominids that frequented the place had a look of far away in their eyes. They ate without passion and did not partake of chat. There was no confab from us either and I observed a stiffness of body from Wirt and Marcellus. I attempted to engage them in talk, but they did not respond and stared hard at their food.

"Do not mind them, Adara, they did not sleep well," Eagard said. "We share one quite small room. The beds are shoved close together and every out breath could be heard. I fear that my snoring may have contributed to their most disagreeable mood."

Wirt snorted. "I hope yer lessons march on a pace. I do not relish the prospect of lying down with these two windbags for too much longer. It was like sleeping with wolfies."

"We not make noise like beast," Marcellus said.

"Ye do. Not as loud, but at a pitch that fairly grates upon the ear."

"We put up with twitching and turning from you. We not complain."

"Really Marcellus? Ye just did."

"Not so."

"Did."

"Not."

"Calm, calm. It is always a test when those not acquainted are forced to share such confined space. Let us now make a pact to attempt to repose in a quiet and serene manner."

Wirt and Marcellus looked into each other's eyes and did not blink. Eadgard sighed and shook his head. I leaned close all conspiratorial and whispered, "What do think these other non-godlys are doing here?"

At my words all turned their attention upon the fems and males that were eating silently on the other table.

"They do not look a friendly bunch. Not one has made an effort to commune with any of the others."

"Perhaps they are here to find peace and restoration from some pain suffered in their life," I said.

"Or maybe spies. Adara, look around. Much here is of interest. Much here defy rules. Much here mystery. Also, books. Sister Gabriel know more than she tell."

I bit my lip so as not to expose my late night encounter with said nun and sat back. Marcellus's words gave me over to thoughts of doubt and anxiety.

"Now, Marcellus, try not to cause concern where there is no foundation. Adara, Wirt, these people most likely are here on route to somewhere else. As are we and we are not spies," Eadgard said.

"You sure?" Marcellus said and Wirt pushed his plate away from him.

"Ye are full of accusations about others. Maybe ye are a spy?"

"Calm again, please. Such rumour only causes distress. Free you mind from such thoughts and finish you grub. Adara? May we have the pleasure of your company at mid-morning?"

"For sure and certain of it."

"Need you to go back to Brother Jude?"

"What? Oh, yep. That I must. Ta for the reminder. Wirt, Marcellus, it would be a great relief to me to know that you will not clash again. Can you agree on that?"

They folded their arms and looked hard at each other. Then slow as slow they relaxed their rigid demeanour and nodded their heads. I took my leave and headed towards the room of learning, not quite as enthused about my lesson as I had been earlier.

I clip-clopped up the winding stairs with less vigour than before and not knowing why, hesitated before opening the door. I thought I heard Brother Jude speaking with someone else and lingered discreetly until he finished. When no more noise emitted, I walked in expecting to find Brother Dominic, but to my amazement he was alone.

"Adara, here you are. All fed and fresh to learn?"

"Keen enough."

"You seem distracted. Has there been an occurrence?"

"Nope. Just that I imagined you engaged in blab when I stood outside."

"No. Perhaps I mumbled some thoughts out loud, but as you can see, I do not have a visitor."

"Quite so. I must have mistaken what I heard."

"It happens. Now shall we proceed?"

"Yep."

"Good. Now you will breathe with continuous air and make the sounds that disturb and soothe, depending on the pitch you choose."

Brother Jude set me to task and I spent many long moments standing, sucking in air, holding it in my cheeks, blowing it out whilst breathing more in and so on until I made the action so smooth that I no longer could tell the difference between breath coming in and breath going out.

All a-woozy from the rush of oxy to my brain, I leant against the wall before continuing. Brother Jude smiled and nodded his head saying, "Good, good, good. You learn fast and well. Mind not the dizziness, it will pass with practice. After your midday meal we will make sound out of this continuous breath."

A loud and resonant bell chimed and Brother Jude pressed his finger to his lips. "Quiet now for prayers. You may go and return when the second bell sounds."

I bowed, not knowing why, except that it seemed the right thing to do, and left. My descent down the stairs was faster and lighter of foot than the previous ascent.

When I reached the library I was surprised to find it inhabited by other folk. Some monks and fem monks sat a table, heads bent, rocking back and forth and muttering words in an ancient tongue low and barely audible. I searched the room and was pleased to observe Wirt, Marcellus and Sister Gabriel sitting round a table attending to something of interest in a book that lay open before them. I spied Eadgard hunched over another tome, with a look of absolute concentration upon his face. So engrossed were all four, that they did not notice my approach.

"All hi and hi again," I said and spread my arms across the shoulders of Wirt and Marcellus. They jumped up and knocked back their chairs, creating a flurry of movement from Sister Gabriel, who faster than a bolt of lightning, snatched the book from the table and hugged it to her chest. Eadgard too stood, brushed his book onto the floor and placed his foot upon it.

"Calmly chums. It is only myself come as requested."

"Adara, ye nearly stopped me heart."

"Not intentionally, Wirt. Why so skittish?"

"The book we are perusing is not for the eyes of all."

"Continue on."

"Book holds answers. Book explains many things. Things we thought one way, discover is other way. Hidden. Truths obscured, answers obtained."

"To what?"

"Come, Adara, sit with me and I shall reveal more."

"Sister Gabriel," Eadgard said and picked up the book he was standing on.

"Might it be better to keep our learning's quieter."

"Quite so," she said and took the tome from his hand.

Another loud ringing put an end to our conversation. Just when it was becoming all-full of interest and intrigue. I noticed those that wore religious garb stop their chanting, rise and shuffle out as though an invisible hand pushed them from behind. The more I saw of this place, the more I became wary.

"You must go to Brother Jude my dear," Sister Gabriel said, opened her eyes wide and pushed her neck out.

"Erhm? What about..?" I stopped my questioning and turned to see Brother Dominic. He stood at the entrance and nodded to all that passed him in a kindly manner. His presence gave meaning to Sister Gabriel's oddly pose.

"That was the bell to end the prayer session," she said in a loud voice that all could hear.

"Oh, right."

"Until later, my dear," Sister Gabriel said and brushed my hand with hers. I felt something being pushed under my fingers and realised it was a note. I scrunched it up into my palm so that it was hidden, and said, "Yeah, I wish all a goodly day."

The others smiled and for a moment I thought I saw a look of glaze come over their eyes. I yawned, strolled past Brother Dominic and out into the corridor that led to Brother Jude.

CHAPTER 24
The Book of Revelations

I walked until Brother Dominic was no longer in sight and opened the note that Sister Gabriel gave me. She had written instructions for me to go all quick to the library. I was intrigued and strode fast to the place of meeting.

She was waiting outside and gestured for me to follow where she was rapidly going, which was towards the front entrance. I kept up with her long strides until we stopped by the large door. She turned to me and said, "Ah, what a glorious day. I'm sure Brother Jude will not mind so much if you and I partake of a quick stroll outside. Come, take my arm and we shall meander for a few secs."

I gave forth a grin most superficial and together we stepped into the mid-morning sun.

"There is a lovely enclosed garden to the side of the property that you must see my dear," Sister Gabriel said. She put her hands inside her enormous pockets and veered to the left of the structure. I took the opportunity, whilst walking beside her, to take in the outside environment. I'd not seen it since we arrived and to tell the truth, did not take so much notice as I should.

I had not realised the vastness of the building until now. It seemed to loom as tall as the mountains that surrounded it. I looked to my right and near gasped at how near I was to the edge of the cliff. I took several steps away from the mist-drenched precipice and stared all squint-eyed at the Monastery. The white walls seemed to shimmer in the sunlight. It was a cheery sight for sure and my feeling of wooziness began to disperse. I shielded my eyes from the dazzle of the building, tilted my head back and fairly wrenched my neck looking up so high to the turreted top; which boasted the strangest figures I had ever seen.

On each corner of said turret were stone effigies of giant hunched-up creatures. They had long, pointed ears and wide-open mouths, with tongues that protruded between oversized fangs. Their eyes were merely deep, empty hollows that saw nowt. They appeared neither hominid nor animal, but a bit of both combined.

"Why such embellishments?"

"Gargoyles, my dear. Relics from the past. They simply represent good and evil. Emblems to guard against daemons and the like."

I thought them splendid, but not so much as the place Sister Gabriel took me to. At first I thought it an extension of the outer wall, being it was just that, a wall. It had a door in the middle with carvings of all sorts of fauna and flora. I ran my fingers across the raised shapes and felt beaks, claws, petals and thorns.

"What grand designs. What expertise in craftsmanship."

"Indeed, my dear. There are those who do have a gift for art and the like. Come, let us enter," Sister Gabriel said and pulled on a large round metal handle that resembled an intertwined garland. The portal creaked open and we stepped through it into a wondrous place indeed.

Tears of awe brimmed full in my eyes and I had to blink more than once to clear them. Flowers and shrubs and trees and grasses covered the walls. More plants and twisty coloured ivy swarmed over and between the arched wooden structures that made a scented covered pathway that we walked along. I breathed in the sweet-sweet smell and fondled leaves so smooth I too wished my skin possessed such silky softness. Sister Gabriel smiled at the sight of my beaming face and allowed a stop for me to revel in the gloriousness of the scene.

"Sister, what sumptuous plants abound here. All green and flowery despite the newness of the season."

"Well, the shrubs and trees are evergreens and the flowers early bloomers. As the spring gives way to summer and so on, so the plants give forth their glory in tune with the changes in weather. It is a place of beauty and serenity to be sure."

"The so-called 'Park' in Cityplace shrivels into insignificance. The paltry flora that survive in that venue is sickly and fragile in comparison. I could give up all thoughts of rescue to abide in such a place, it enchants me so."

"Though I am gratified at your pleasure in this garden, my dear, I would not have you dismiss your purpose for the scent and sight of pretty things. Come, we are nearly at our destination," she said and steered me towards a high green hedge, all but obscured from the rest of the place. We hurried behind it and I saw Eadgard, Wirt and Marcellus sitting at a round wooden table. They turned their faces to me and I thought I saw a look of deep concern on each and every one.

"What can be so unpleasant that you scowl in a place of such beauty?"

"Sit my dear, there is something I must show you."

I did as Sister Gabriel instructed and attempted a smile to ease the air of gloom that pervaded. Eadgard reached down and picked up the book that I had seen in the library but a few secs ago. He slapped it onto the table, opened it and shoved it across to where I sat. He pointed at an image and said, "That pic shows genetically designed hominids being mass produced."

I stared at the thing and shrugged. "So? We know that occurred. Hardly a secret."

"But not on the scale that is mentioned here. This pic was taken in 2092."

"What? So far back? But-"

"There is more. The text goes on to reveal the reason for such a deed. A year after the great world famine in 2085, humanity suffered an even greater threat. A drought of such magnitude that nearly all died."

"No, it wasn't a drought, it was a plague."

"No, Adara," Sister Gabriel said.

She sat next to me, turned the page and pressed her finger down on an image showing thousands of corpses strewn across roadways, city pavements and crop-withered fields. She showed more. A pic of a mighty wave engulfing an entire city. Then another showing bodies both hominid, animal and fish, floating lifeless on the surface of the water.

"You see, my dear, the place that once was Great Britain succumbed to rising seas that shrunk it to its present size. Land was scarce and many died in the battle to own it. Judging from the state of things now, it would appear that the Agros won."

"How is it we do not know of this? This history was not taught at my learning place."

"Such truth was hidden my dear, by those who wished to control and benefit from the despair that was left."

"Agros."

"And Scientists. They ruled what was left of humanity. I have read other more disturbing facts. There is a book that contains fragments of official documents from the time. It was hidden in the library. I found it only yesterday and I can tell you it is as well it was kept secret, for in it is evidence that Agros ordered the mass destruction of all who refused to surrender to their tyrannical rule."

I looked to Wirt. He hung his head. I turned to Marcellus and Eadgard, but neither was able to meet my gaze. I shook my noggin and felt it would surely burst from all this dreadful news, when Sister Gabriel pulled out two small black books from her extensive pockets.

"These are said books," she said and placed them onto the table before me. She opened one and I stared at the page with uneasy eyes. I saw amongst the plethora of words and mathematical symbols, pics of mutated creatures. Some resembled animals, but not any that I have seen in other mags or vids, and some were most definitely hominid in appearance.

Although head and limbs were often not in the places I was used to seeing them. She flicked sheet after sheet, showing me more and more of the freakish images, until she came to one particular page. I sat back and looked to the others.

"What does this mean, these grotesque pics of things that should not exist?"

"These, my dear, are the early trials at cloning. As far back as 1996 scientists were able to successfully clone mammals. After that, well, they left caution to the wind and cloned all sorts of creatures. Goats with DNA of spiders that produced silk in their milk. Pigs cloned with human cells that could be used in organ transplants. And as you have observed in these photopics, humans and animals cloned to produce hybrid monsters. For what purposes? War. These," she said and pointed to a thing that resembled a male only without much in the way of features to speak of, "these were called 'Ultimate Warriors.'"

Their faces were alarming to behold. There were dark holes where eyes should have been; two slanted slashes in the middle of the face were I suppose, nostrils and the small round orifice in between them, a mouth. Their arms were so muscle bound that they stuck out from their shoulders, making it look as though they were about to flap them and take flight. As for the legs, they were short, stumpy almost and just as brawny as the other limbs. The whole effect was that of brute and then some.

I pulled the book away from her and looked through it. Each page showed images of all manner of hybrid monsters. There was a series of pics that were truly dreadful. They showed an army of "Ultimate

Warriors" destroying whole cities. Tearing out the throats of the inhabitants and laying waste to the buildings with explosive devices so powerful that all that remained was rubble. I closed the book and hung my head. I felt a hand touch mine, looked up and saw Wirt.

"The second book has more to tell. Although the pics are not so unpleasant, the content is shocking none the less."

"You have seen this, Wirt?"

"Aye, we all have."

"Show me then."

Sister Gabriel handed me the other black book. With shaking fingers I opened it. There on the front cover was a pic of a Clonie with the words "Reject: banish with the rest. Rations for two months then no more. If any survive after that time- kill them all."

Marcellus wiped his eyes and I knew by that gesture that he recognised his own ancestors.

"We did not die. We survived. We fought and still fight to remain alive. Agros still treat us like experiments, we used like lab rats for their research."

"Turn the page, my dear."

I did and saw to my horror pics of folk that I seemed to recognise. I stared at Wirt and Eadgard and Sister Gabriel and said, "They could be related to you and yours. See Wirt, the same hair, eye colour and stumpy thumb as you have. Here Eadgard are your long fingers and big-big ears, and here, here Sister I see the perfect features you show to us each day. And here, the softly skin and slender shape of all in Cityplace, except perhaps for me. I am confused beyond confusedness to be sure."

"Adara, we are not only Clonies on land," Marcellus said. "We, you-related."

I let my mouth hang open for a moment then looked around at my companions. A sudden thought occurred to me and a smile inched its way across my face. I waggled a forefinger at them all.

"Did you fashion this flimflam tale to dupe me and create much mirth at my expense?"

Sister Gabriel lowered her gaze and clasped her hands before her. Then she spoke in a soft low tone, "We are not tricking you, my dear. These words and images distress and confuse but they are true. These books were hidden in a secret place. I watched Brother Augustus and saw him locate said tomes, then stole them before he could make sense of their contents. I kept all out of sight until now. It was more than I could bear to keep such important info from you."

I caught my breath and felt my heartbeat quicken.

"What does this all mean?"

The others sat and Wirt took my hand. Eadgard coughed and Marcellus stared into my eyes. Sister Gabriel raised her head and sat upright in her seat.

"It means, my dear, that we could all be described as Clonies, since it would appear that we have the same identical ancestors. Granted over the years the genetic coding has weakened. Your extra digits are proof of that, and your extraordinary vocal talent - a thing the Agros may be rather keen on."

"Adara is in danger then?"

"Yes, Wirt, I would suggest that is a strong possibility."

I pulled my hands away from Wirt and stared at my fingers, all twelve of them. I had not given much thought to their difference until now. I believed that I was not the only fem with such an extra appendage, but it seemed that I was. Now all was confusion and strangeness. Now, I was unsure of everything.

"You must go to Brother Jude, my dear. I have kept you too long. Think of what we have discovered but do not speak of it, not even to him."

"No fear. I have no desire to repeat the things gleaned in this most precious place," I said and rose. Although my belly jumped and turned and my skin prickled all over, I was determined not to blub. I sniffed a bit, nodded to the rest and walked heavy-footed through the tangled walkway, back to the Monastery. My head bent as low as the grumbling clouds that swept across the sky and hid the sun behind a mask of grey.

CHAPTER 25
The Sound of Eternal Rest

I plodded my way up the stone spiral staircase caring not for the lesson that awaited me. I pushed open the door and took a deep breath, ready to commence my learning with Brother Jude. The sight that presented itself to me was a cause of vast befuddlement. Said monk was sitting on a chair speaking into a communications pod. Brother Dominic had told us on our arrival that this place was a place of peace and sanctuary and that only the Abbot had access to chat with the world outside.

Brother Jude raised his head and pressed the screen on his pod.

"Adara, you are late. The bell chimed some time ago. It is of no importance. Come, do not linger by the door. We can resume our lesson. Come, enter."

I did not reply.

"Come, it is time. If you do not enter and commence then you will not learn. If you do not learn-"

"What? What will happen if I do not complete my studies?"

"Do you not wish to?"

"I did, 'tis true, but now I am not so sure."

"Pray explain yourself."

"Pray you explain yourself," I said and folded my arms.

"I do not know what you mean."

"You were chatting on a pod."

Brother Jude said nothing.

"Your silence confirms my hunch all right. I recall being told that only the Abbott himself had such a device."

As soon as I mentioned the Abbot something seemed to switch back on in my head. I blinked, wiped my eyes and stared over his head and out of the window. The clouds that had followed me all the way to the Monastery, dispersed and melted into nothing. The sun shone bright and clear and I said, "The Abbot. Why have we not yet seen him?"

Brother Jude lifted himself from his chair and walked slowly towards me. He had a smile that was not so pleasant and did not fill me with confidence or calm. I backed away, turned and ran down the steps.

Before I reached the bottom, I heard a sound so savage and raw that my head felt as if a knife was being thrust into it. I grabbed onto my noggin and squeezed my eyes tight shut. The sound intensified. I felt the deep, low tones shudder throughout my bod and shake it so that I thought an earthquake was about to explode under my feet. I sank onto the stone step and Brother Jude let loose another noise bomb. I put my hands over my ears to try and block out the din, but it grew louder. I rocked back and forth wishing for the hideous drone to stop. It did not. I tried to stand, to move away, but a hand gripped my shoulder and dug in so much that it felt as if the muscles were being torn away from my bones.

Brother Jude twisted me around, knelt and put his leering gob close to mine.

"I have waited too long for you to let you fall from my grasp." I felt his hot breath against my cheek, and would have turned my head away but could not. Try as I might I was unable to move and had to listen to his filthy words slide down my ears.

"I will tempt you away from your true calling. I will manipulate your talent to serve my purpose. I no longer care for the Agro assignment they gave me. I know you. I know your true potential. I will have it for myself. You will come with me and finish your lesson. Or here where you sit, will be your last resting place. For if I cannot have what you have, then you are as nothing to me."

I conjured up all that was left of my strength and spat into his contorted face. He sat back on his heels, wiped off the spittle and stood. "Wolfbitch," he said, bent down, grabbed my wrist and yanked. I tried to resist, to pull away but he tightened his grip. I thought he would rip my hand right off. I wriggled and twisted as best I could, but I was no match against the weight of sound that he channelled towards me.

His mouth opened wide, his eyes bulged and his tongue stuck out. I was reminded of the gargoyles outside and once again attempted to free myself. But the guttural, razor sound that issued from his throat was too powerful. It swelled inside my head and kept me stuck to the floor. His hands slipped underneath my armpits. I was all limp and squishy and could not resist. He lifted me a tad and dragged me up the staircase step-by-step. He never ceased the abominable sound, even though his laboured breath came out hard and fast.

My desire to be free from his clutches grew with every bump to my rear. I forced all other thoughts from my head and focused on escape. Although my body was his to command, my mind was made of stronger stuff. I concentrated hard and harder still on my friends and pictured all their faces. I remembered everything that Brother Jude had taught me. How to breathe in order to make my notes last longer; how to call forth things by identifying their individual frequencies and singing only to them. The way I had brought back the chickle and summoned the eagle. I focused on the 'dult who was hauling me up the steps as if I was no more than a sac of apples, and listened to who he was. Through the nastiness that spewed from his mouth, I heard an inside note. A thin and mewling moan that was his true persona.

With one greatly effort I filled my hunched up lungs with air and let out a sound all squeaky high. A sissy noise that he recognised at once. I made it again and Brother Jude came to a halt. He stiffened for a sec, pulled my shoulders up to my ears, then shuddered all violent-like and let me go. I tumbled down bashing head and bum on stone, and landed all scrunched up at the bottom of the stairs.

"Adara? Adara? Are ye alive?"

I opened my eyes to see Wirt's face above my own.

"Alive, I think."

"Marcellus and I came when we heard ye sing. Such a thin and feeble note, that we became all concerned. What has occurred?"

I gulped and held up my arms. Wirt grabbed onto
my forearms and pulled, but I was still a leaden lump
and could not move enough for him to lift me. Wirt
turned his head and called out to Marcellus. I steered
my gaze to where he looked and saw Marcellus
hasten down the bleak passageway to where I lay. He
took my hands and gently pulled me to my feet. I
leant against his chest and felt the quickness of his
heartbeat match my own.

"Brother Jude?" I said and broke free of
Marcellus's welcome embrace. His big hand gripped
mine and we took a few steps to the alcove. He leant
his head inside and looked upwards.

"I see body hunched. I think crying. You fear for
him?"

"Nope. I am a-feared of him."

Marcellus pulled back his head and looked into
my eyes. "He harm you?"

I nodded. His face darkened and he clenched his
hands into fists.

"We have sense that all is awry. We take you
from this place to other more secure."

He took my elbow and made to move away, but I
stopped him by yanking my mitt free of his and
slumping to the ground, head in hands. A spike of
pain dug into my brain. A stabbing sensation that
slowly turned into a sound, that in turn became a
word. That in turn became a name. Lost in the
fugginess of my addled noggin it repeated until I
could contain it no longer.

I opened my mush and said as loud as I could,
"Abbot. Abbot!"

I said the name again and again and saw both
Wirt and Marcellus blink all quick-like, as if to wash

away some grit. I was compelled to speak the word and did so over and over. I became stronger with each mention of his moniker and stood tall and straight. I walked past my friends and into the corridor. I breathed in and said the name twice more.

"Abbot. Abbot."

At the far end of the passage I saw the figures of Eadgard and Sister Gabriel running at full pelt and shouting something that I could not quite make out. I waved to them but they did not wave back. They hurtled towards me as if being followed by something mean. I observed that behind them scurried all those that we had shared the place of eating with. And all without exception were shouting the name "Abbot" with such volume that it ceased to be a word at all and became as like a bolt of lightning that shot into our very hearts.

I placed my hands over my ears and was about to say something like "what's with all the name calling?" when they stopped dead. Sister Gabriel, who was no more than a bubs length from me, made a face as if she were chewing raw onions. Eadgard, put a hand to her shoulder but pulled it away all sharpish and grasped onto the sides of his head. I watched as all the folk next to and around them screwed up their faces and grabbed at their chests. I heard all let out a great gasp. They choked for a sec then everyone before me fell down. I turned to witness Wirt and Marcellus clutch at their chests and collapse to the floor. I took my hands away from my ears, hurried to my friends and knelt beside them.

"Wirt?" I said and touched his cheek. It was cold.

"Marcellus?" He did not answer.

I rose and stared at the crumpled bodies on the ground. I walked to where Sister Gabriel and Eadgard lay and squatted beside them. I bent my head towards their mouths and heard nowt. There came a silence that was so quiet, I felt it on my skin. Something warm trickled down my jawline. I put my hand to my face and wiped away the blood that oozed from my ear and stood.

"Still conscious, Adara? Well done."

Through the carnage on the floor walked Brother Dominic. He took something plug-like from his ears and clapped his hands as if to suggest that I had performed something of wonder. He stepped over the prostrate figures not once glancing down to see who was underfoot.

"You really are The One. Brother Jude was right. Speaking of which, where is he?"

"I left him somewhere upon the steps."

"Dead or alive?"

"Alive I believe. Although I wish it were not so."

"Good. Not so much damage done then."

He held out his hand for me to take but I brushed it aside and stepped back to where Wirt and Marcellus lay. I saw how pale their faces had become and felt an iciness creep throughout my body. Brother Dominic squinted and pursed his lips.

"You should be amongst this rabble. You should be as close to death as these," he said and produced a small object that looked like something I had seen in a history vid. It was a dark disc with a long stick-like thing jutting out of it. I rummaged in my addled brain to access where and in what context I had seen it before.

"All I need to do is to click this switch to full power and you and all of these expendables will be no more," Brother Dominic said and pointed the thing at me.

"An ultra sonic gun. That is a relic and no mistake."

"Still works though. A fine weapon it is too, made in the first part of the twenty-first to control angry mobs. Supposedly non-lethal, but then someone used it to do more harm than good and it was discredited as dangerous and banned."

He smirked and twiddled with a dial on the side of the handle. "On this setting, the brain seizures causing instant death."

I was all-thankful that my instinct for survival had kicked in when it did, or that thing would have scuppered me as well. My nonce all tutored up from Brother Jude's lessons, blocked out the higher than high frequency and I remained awake. But I was not so sure that at a more intense level I could withstand its devastating power.

"This device you have used on all of these?"

"Indeed, but on a safer setting."

"Why? Why do such dreadful stuff?"

"To stop you from continuing your journey to free the Meeks. What you have learned from the traitor Sister Gabriel is information best kept secret. This knowledge is a danger to us, to the Agro plans for all of humankind."

"But you are holy men and women. How can you..?"

"Stifle your curiosity, Adara, it is of little use. Know this before you die, that neither Brother Jude nor myself are true believers. Like you we are on a quest. But that has changed. Thanks to the good sister there," he said and poked her in the ribs with his foot. He gave me a most unpleasant grin and raised the weapon level to my face.

"I have devised a new mission. To end your existence and keep safe the secret Sister Gabriel chose to reveal. I realise that the Agros will question your demise. They had plans for you. But when I tell them that you found out the truth about their schemes, they will understand that what I am about to do was a necessity."

He placed his finger on the switch at the side of the handle, just below the black disc. He paused for a moment and said, "I will allow you to pray to whatever or whomever you believe in. But make it quick, I would have an end to this."

He squinted and aimed the gun at my head.

I closed my eyes and waited for the sound that would end the thumping in my chest.

CHAPTER 26
Open Mouthed

Quite a few secs went by and I heard nowt. No skull smashing sound that would turn my brain to squish. No noise that would send a shock wave coursing through my bod to burst my vitals. Nowt, nadder, not a thing.

I opened my eyes and saw Brother Dominic staring at the floor. The sonic gun pushed down between his belt and robe. I gulped and he lifted his gaze.

"Don't look so perplexed. Or for that matter, relieved. I haven't forgot that I am to kill you. I just thought I'd have a little fun first."

He bent over Eadgard and Sister Gabriel and shoved them close together. He positioned their heads in such a way as to make them look as if they were about to kiss, then stood and faced me. He pulled the weapon from his belt, held it up and pointed it at my noggin.

"I will arrange your corpse on top of that Clonie filth when I am done. And that irregular youth, Wirt, whom you choose to call friend, I will place on top of you. Thus making a sandwich out of freak."

His words and actions sent coldness around my innards. A cold that burned. I became as vexed as I had in the Nearlyman camp and felt a fury rise within. I directed my stare and thoughts upon Brother Dominic and Jude. I partook of the biggest breath I could, and made a sound low and hard. So deep and sonorous that the windows began to rattle.

Brother Dominic looked around, screwed his faced up in pain and dropped the ultrasonic gun. It crashed to the floor and split in two. He clasped his hands to the sides of his head and opened his mouth, but no sound came out. I let forth a final surge of guttural resonance that sent him shooting backwards to the end of the corridor. He hit the wall and fell splat onto the ground. I heard behind and above my head a similar thud and guessed that it was from the slumping of Brother Jude. I stopped and breathed as normal, before taking in more air.

This time it was a sweet lungful and I let my voice cry out a tune of softness and calm. I did not know what, if any effect, it might have upon the stricken, but it felt good to let my voice ring in purity instead of filth. I walked amongst limp arms and legs, crouched down and touched cold face after cold face. When I came upon Eadgard and Sister Gabriel, I pushed them both onto their backs. I lingered by Eadgard's mouth and let my ear listen for sounds of his breathing. I heard nowt. I rose, wiped my eyes and stood straight and strong. I looked over the bods that lay so still on the floor and paused.

Then, I took a breath and sang until my throat could take no more.

Bent double from the effort I sank to my knees and buried my head in my hands. For the first time in my life, I prayed. To the Greenman, the Onegreatbeing and the Babychesus. I prayed for Marcellus, Wirt, Eadgard, Sister Gabriel, and all those that lay near to death to breathe and live again.

When I'd done, I lifted my head. No one moved. I leant over Eadgard and to my wonder and delight I saw his face take on a colour more suited to life than death. I turned to Sister Gabriel and she too had a pinkness where before was only pallor. I rose and stepped between bod after bod and witnessed the same glow appear upon the dull skin of all that lay unconscious. And when I came to Wirt and Marcellus, I almost let out a girlygig shriek as their lids began to flutter. One by one I witnessed the lifeless open their eyes take in air and slowly get to their feet. Some retched up dryness, some wobbled and shook their heads as if to dispel something stuck inside. Then all stood straight. I saw them through a haze of bafflement, for I did not know just what had occurred. My mouth felt all scratchy and dry, but there was a cleanness of taste instead of bitter bile. I rubbed my eyes and blinked a bit and saw the floored folk slowly come to life.

They moved their arms first, raising one then the other high above their heads. Shoulders wriggled and faces contorted in pain then relief as blood flowed with a quicker force than before. My head tingled as my wits were restored. It felt as if a clammy hand had been lifted from my brain and the world and what I must do became clear once more.

I stared at the dazed monks, nuns and other folk and they too lost their look of dumb. I saw them twitch and turn and babble to themselves, then at each other, until a low murmur swept throughout the risen. I'd not heard such noise in all the time of our stay. The silence that had been became a roar of thanks that turned to anger as more and more became aware that something wrong had occurred. It was not a foul sound but a defiant one that caused a swell in my chest. I smiled at Eadgard and he gave me the thumbs-up sign. He stared into Sister Gabriel's eyes and she squeezed his forearm and nodded to the others. Eadgard, protector that he was, went amongst the folk checking for injuries and chatting to one and all.

I approached Sister Gabriel. "Sister, what has been and gone here?"

"An underhandedness of high proportion, my dear."

I folded my arms and cocked my head to one side. Although glad at her rejuvenation, Brother Dominic's words of her duplicity lingered in my nonce.

"Indeed a deception of the highest order, of which I am told you were to have contributed?" I said.

Sister Gabriel sighed and looked to the ceiling, then gave me one of her piecing stares.

"Listen not to the words of those who are so devious."

I was about to ask her to clarify, but my attention was drawn away from said nun by the sight of Wirt and Marcellus walking towards us. I could not help hugging both to my chest. Neither pulled away and it was Eadgard who finally parted our reunion by saying, "We were all sitting in the place of eating

when we heard Brother Dominic chant the word
'Abbot.' Then all went black, until I heard you call to
me."

I took his hand and we partook of a relief-filled
grin. From the corner of my eye, I saw the newly
risen folk approach, all eagerly chatting as though
they had been asleep for many moons. They stopped
in a huddle before me and their banter ceased. A
young grey robed monk stepped forward and bowed.

"You are a wonder. May I take it upon myself to
give you thanks for restoring us all to rightfulness?"

"Thanks accepted with the grace given.
However, I did nothing to aid your recovery other
than-"

"Other than what?" the monk said.

I lowered my eyes. "Other than pray."

"We are relieved to be free from the seeming
spell we have been under since our arrival."

"Which was when?" Eadgard said.

"That I cannot say. I am guessing some goodly
time and then some."

I felt a hand touch my elbow and turned.

"Adara, Where Brother Dominic?" Marcellus
said.

I pointed at the far wall.

"He lies senseless at the end of this corridor. He
aimed that sound weapon at me on full potential and I
felt a compulsion to prevent him from using it," I said
and chin gestured to where said thing lay. Sister
Gabriel hurried to where it was, picked it up and
pushed the two separate pieces together. It clicked,
and I swear the thing was all restored.

"How you do this Adara?"

"Well, Marcellus, I used my voice. Brother Jude, although a baddy, as it turns out, schooled me well."

"Now you are the weapon I think, my dear," Sister Gabriel said and peered at the deadly object. "This he kept a secret. But not the dope he put into the food to keep everyone placid."

"I knew it must be drugs. All this while here and not knowing why or what we are about. 'Twas if we were all dreaming. The Abbot too?" the youthful monk said.

"The Abbot. Why I had almost forgot about him. He was the reason for our visit," Eadgard said.

"And the reason we are all here. He must be found. Without his guidance we are as nothing," the juve monk said.

I saw the assembled folk lower their heads and felt a waft of hopelessness spread amongst us all. I looked to my friends but each one shook their head, except for Sister Gabriel.

"Although I do not know for sure. I believe I have an inkling as to where Brother Dominic and Jude may have secreted him."

"When the time is right, Sister Gabriel," Eadgard said and bent close to her. "I would have words with you concerning your involvement in all this chicanery."

"Dear Eadgard, set your mind at ease. I never was a part of their plot. When mention of spies abounded our conversation, it was I who should have come clean. I work for those who wish to prevent the Agros and Scientists from completing their intent."

"Which is?" I said and sidled up close to her.

"Ah, now if we knew that, then all would be quite different," she said and pulled off her face and neck covering. Eadgard's eyes widened at the sight of sister Gabriel's long red hair falling all a-bouncy around her shoulders, quite changing her outward appearance from shifty to sultry. Those gathered around us put their hands to their mouths and stepped back.

"Ye are a Lady." Wirt cried, grabbed one of her hands and held it up to show us all. "See? See her perfect fingers? I would guesstimate she has not a blotch or blemish or nowt about her bod that would show her to be as we are."

"What a perceptive creature you are, dear, Wirt. A Lady, you are half right. But those that look at the floor right now not knowing what to think, may like to understand that we Ladies are more than the sum of our parts."

"More hidden things. More confusion. We not know what to think," Marcellus said and turned away. Eadgard wiped his face with his hand and blinked.

"The finding of the Abbot must be our next priority," he said.

"For sure, my dears, Brother Dominic knows his whereabouts. Adara you must rise him from his stupor."

"This I will try to do, Sister Gabriel, or whoever you are, but I am all concerned that if I waken one then the other will also rise."

Marcellus stepped forward. "We make sure treacherous monk not move." he said and marched off towards the staircase where Brother Jude lay. The non-holy folk came forward. A large male wearing a black skirt not unlike those worn by the Manly's in Wirt's camp addressed us.

"Yer man there is brave, but I reckon could do wi a hand. My nam is Bestanden and I and the other males wi keep yer large pal company," he said and with a wave to the others joined Marcellus.

Wirt took my hand and said, "So, Adara, shall we go to Dominic?"

"A better plan I cannot think of," I said and Wirt, Eadgard and the not quite Sister Gabriel followed me to where he lay sprawled out upon the floor as if a great wind had knocked him over. The monks and nuns that remained in the corridor scuttled over and stood droop-eyed opposite his prostrate form.

"It may be best if you do not linger here. We are not certain of Adara's powers and your safety is of the utmost importance."

"Sister Gabriel is right, although, she is not actually a nun," Eadgard said and folded his arms. He stared at her all squinty-like and she lowered her head. "Exactly who are you?"

Wirt raised his hand bub fashion and said, "She is a Lady and her name is-" He folded his arms and stared with deep intent into the fake Sister's eyes. She stared back and let her mouth turn up at one end as if to suggest Wirt would have a bother to complete his task. "Kendra. That is yer name."

The holy ones stared wide-eyed and forlorn at Kendra. Eadgard sighed and spoke. "This must be a moment of befuddlement beyond any you have encountered."

They nodded.

"May I suggest you all go to the library and there familiarize yourselves with the findings Sister Gabriel, I mean, Kendra, has unearthed?"

They did not move.

"Really, it would be best if you went," Eadgard said and flicked his fingers in the direction of the library.

They remained still.

Eadgard folded his arms.

"Why do you not go?"

The god believers looked at one another and the young monk said, "But sir, the lost books are forbidden to us. We may only read them on the direct instructions of our Brother Abbot."

Kendra pushed her thick hair behind her ears, blinked a slow blink of composure and walked over to where the nuns and monks stood; their eyes lowered, their heads glum-hanging, and said, "My dears, your Brother Abbot is quite out of it. He has not given a direct order for many, many moons. Go, look through the banned books, and learn the things that all should know."

They lifted their weary noggins and stared blankly at Kendra. She smiled, reached out and took the hand of the newbie monk; she placed it into the hand of a juve nun that stood next to him. "Clasp onto one another for support, my dears and do what must be done. The more that know the truth, the better for all."

"You speak wisdom," the young monk said. "Come, brothers and sisters, let us learn that which will make us strong."

The holies blinked and shuffled their feet, then took each other by the hand and strode towards the library.

Kendra folded her arms and gave a goodly sigh. "Ah, they will be much tested with regards to their faith."

I also gave out a cheek-filled blow of air. "That they will and no mistake. What little faith I had in anything became as nowt when I set my eyes on those revealing pages."

Eadgard turned to me with lowered brow and thin lips. "Come, Adara, it is time to rouse Brother Dominic and find the Abbot."

"And when we do?"

Eadgard took both my hands in his and said, "When we do, your true mission will begin."

Armed with an Hons Degree in drama & English literature and a creative writing diploma, **Nicola J. McDonagh** came to writing prose via playwriting. She chose novels as her most recent creative medium because they allow her the freedom to develop character, story, subject matter and interesting use of language.

"For me a good story has to be character driven." Nicola reveals action and plot through how her characters react to situations, and not the other way around. Her writing routine involves sitting down in her comfy, well-loved armchair and completing at least one chapter every afternoon.

Born in Liverpool, Nicola currently resides in a 17th century cottage in mid Suffolk, UK, with her husband and rescue/feral cats. Currently, she's penning the third novel in her *Song of Forgetfulness* series.

Keep tabs on her at FablePress.com or
https://www.facebook.com/thesongofforgetfulness

3664955R00140

Printed in Great Britain
by Amazon.co.uk, Ltd.,
Marston Gate.